Graphic Dickens.

OLIVER TWIST

Retold by Hilary Burningham
Illustrated by Chris Rowlatt

Evans

For Caspar

The author wishes to thank her youthful advisor Joel Francis for his help in the preparation of this book.

Published in 2009 by Evans Brothers Ltd
2A Portman Mansions
Chiltern St
London W1U 6NR

© in the text Hilary Burningham 2009
© in the layout Evans Brothers Ltd 2009

British Library Cataloguing in Publication Data

Burningham, Hilary.
    Oliver Twist. -- (Graphic Dickens)
    1. Orphans--England--London--Comic books, strips, etc.--Juvenile fiction. 2. London (England)--Social conditions--19th century--Comic books, strips, etc.--Juvenile fiction. 3. Children's stories--Comic books, strips, etc.
    I. Title II. Series III. Rowlatt, Chris. IV. Dickens, Charles, 1812-1870.
    741.5-dc22

ISBN: 9780237536541

Editor: Bryony Jones
Designer: Mark Holt

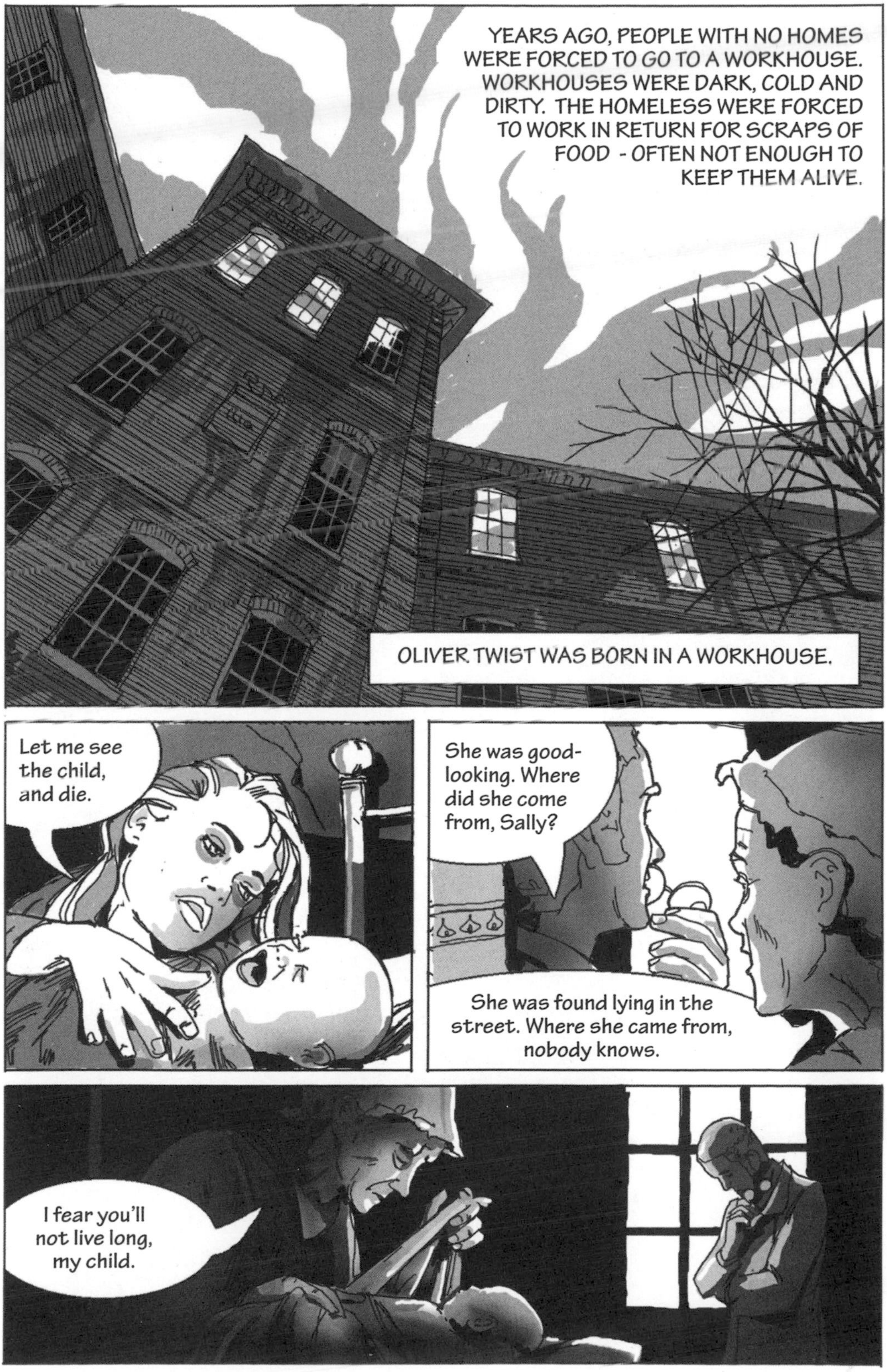
YEARS AGO, PEOPLE WITH NO HOMES WERE FORCED TO GO TO A WORKHOUSE. WORKHOUSES WERE DARK, COLD AND DIRTY. THE HOMELESS WERE FORCED TO WORK IN RETURN FOR SCRAPS OF FOOD - OFTEN NOT ENOUGH TO KEEP THEM ALIVE.
OLIVER TWIST WAS BORN IN A WORKHOUSE.
Let me see the child, and die.
She was good-looking. Where did she come from, Sally?
She was found lying in the street. Where she came from, nobody knows.
I fear you'll not live long, my child.

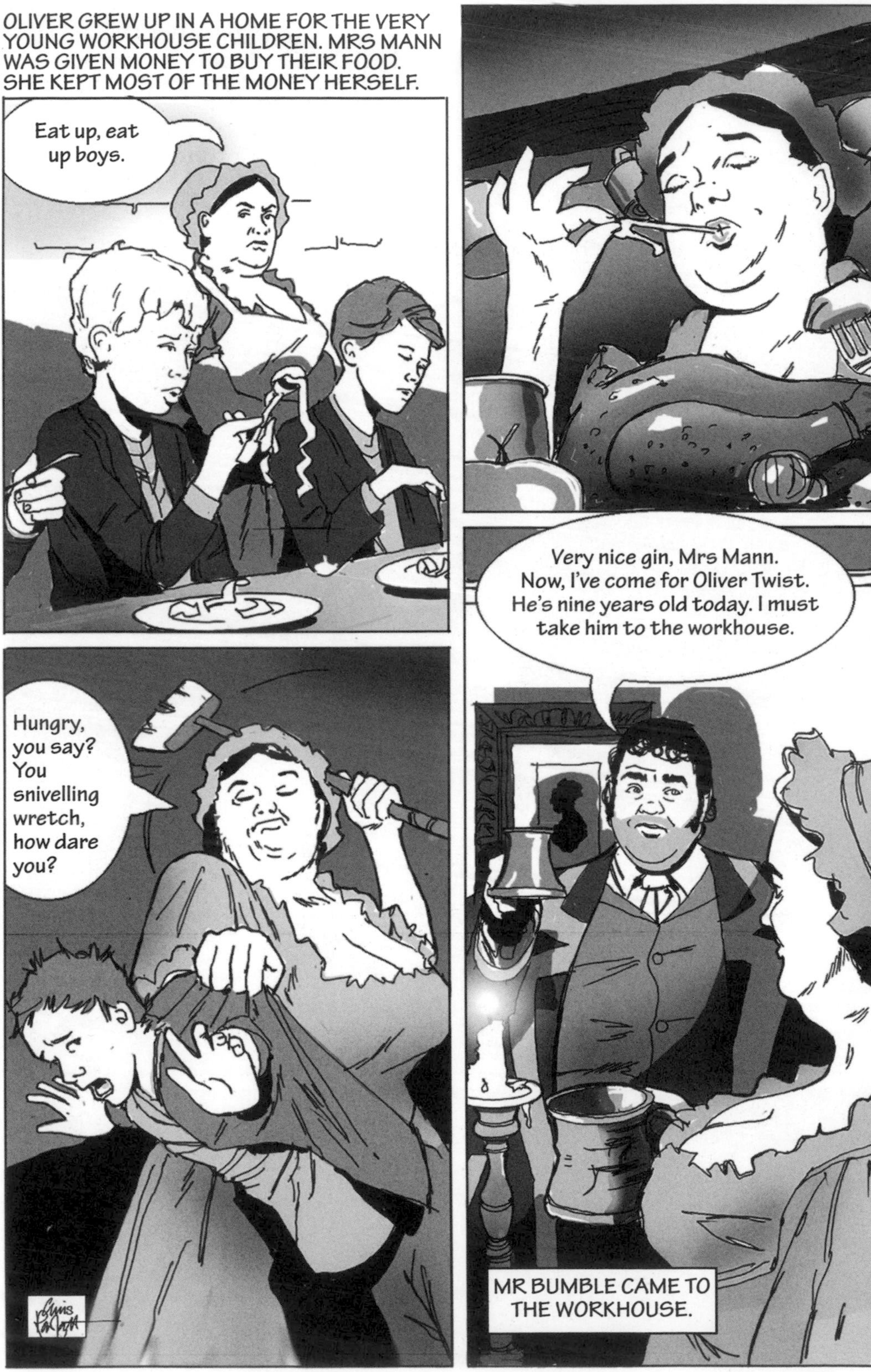
OLIVER GREW UP IN A HOME FOR THE VERY YOUNG WORKHOUSE CHILDREN. MRS MANN WAS GIVEN MONEY TO BUY THEIR FOOD. SHE KEPT MOST OF THE MONEY HERSELF.
Eat up, eat up boys.
Hungry, you say? You snivelling wretch, how dare you?
Very nice gin, Mrs Mann. Now, I've come for Oliver Twist. He's nine years old today. I must take him to the workhouse.
MR BUMBLE CAME TO THE WORKHOUSE.

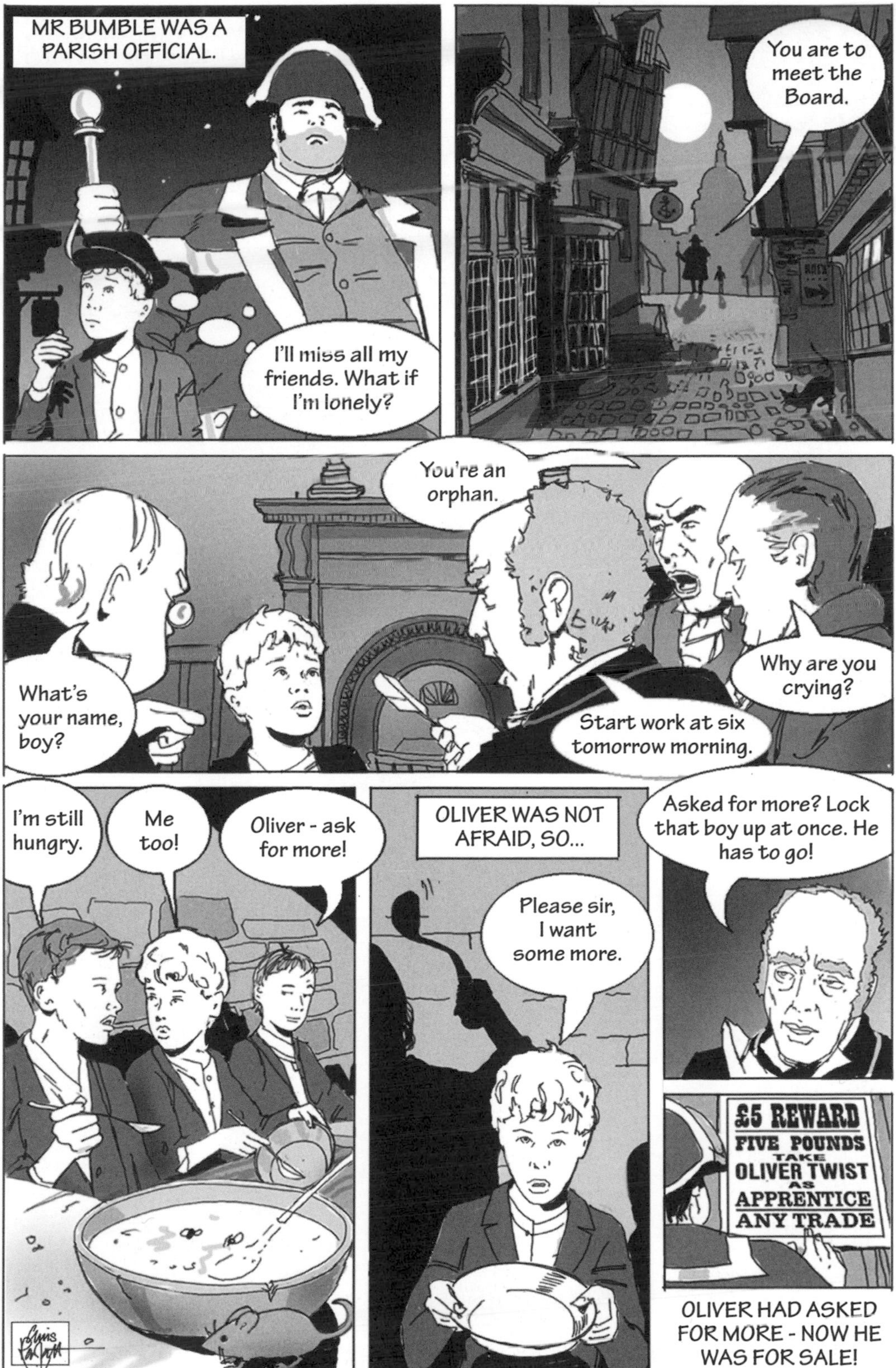
MR BUMBLE WAS A PARISH OFFICIAL.
I'll miss all my friends. What if I'm lonely?
You are to meet the Board.
You're an orphan.
What's your name, boy?
Start work at six tomorrow morning.
Why are you crying?
I'm still hungry.
Me too!
Oliver - ask for more!
OLIVER WAS NOT AFRAID, SO...
Please sir, I want some more.
Asked for more? Lock that boy up at once. He has to go!
£5 REWARD
FIVE POUNDS
TAKE
OLIVER TWIST
AS
APPRENTICE
ANY TRADE
OLIVER HAD ASKED FOR MORE - NOW HE WAS FOR SALE!

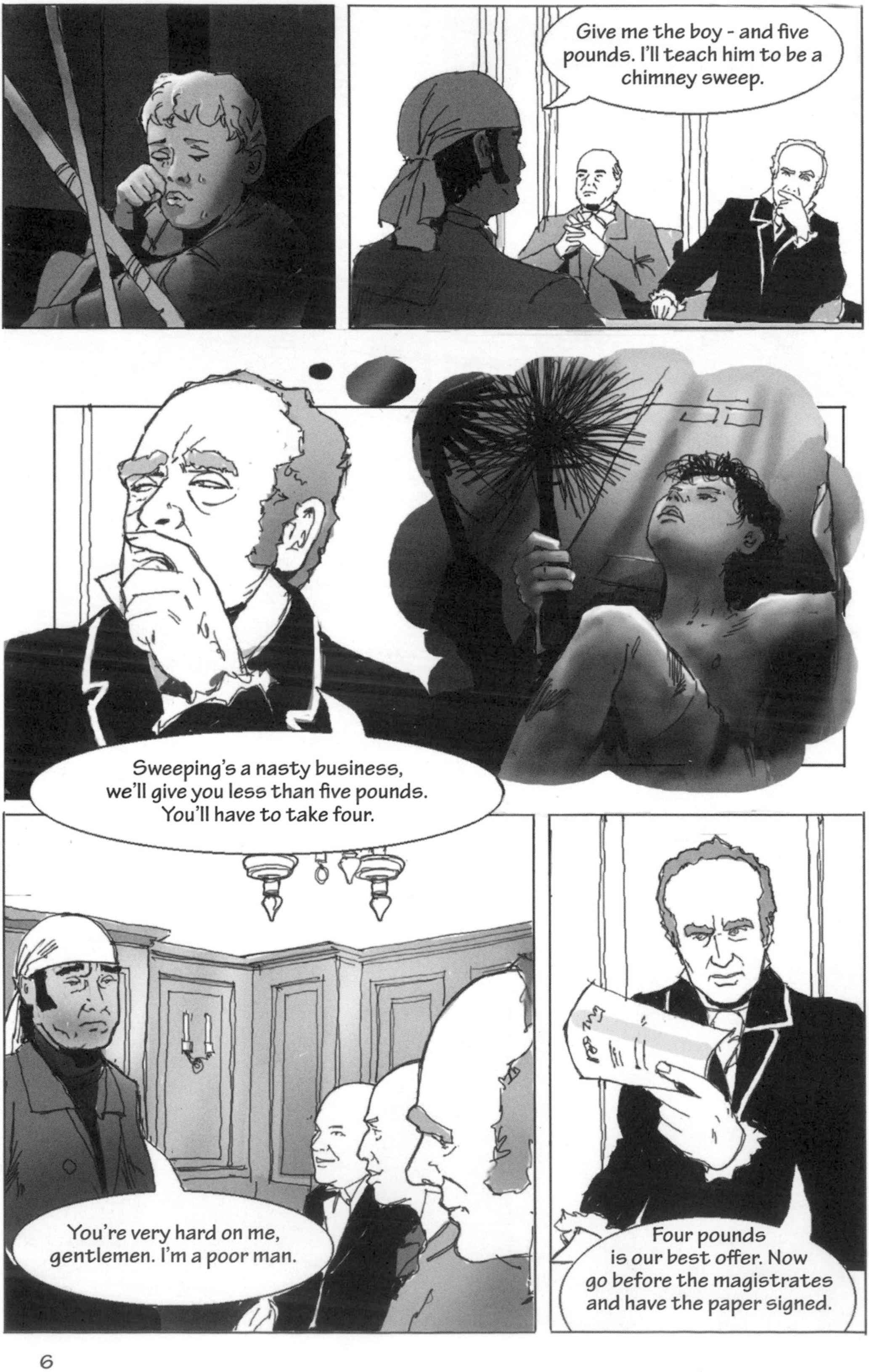
Give me the boy - and five pounds. I'll teach him to be a chimney sweep.
Sweeping's a nasty business, we'll give you less than five pounds. You'll have to take four.
You're very hard on me, gentlemen. I'm a poor man.
Four pounds is our best offer. Now go before the magistrates and have the paper signed.

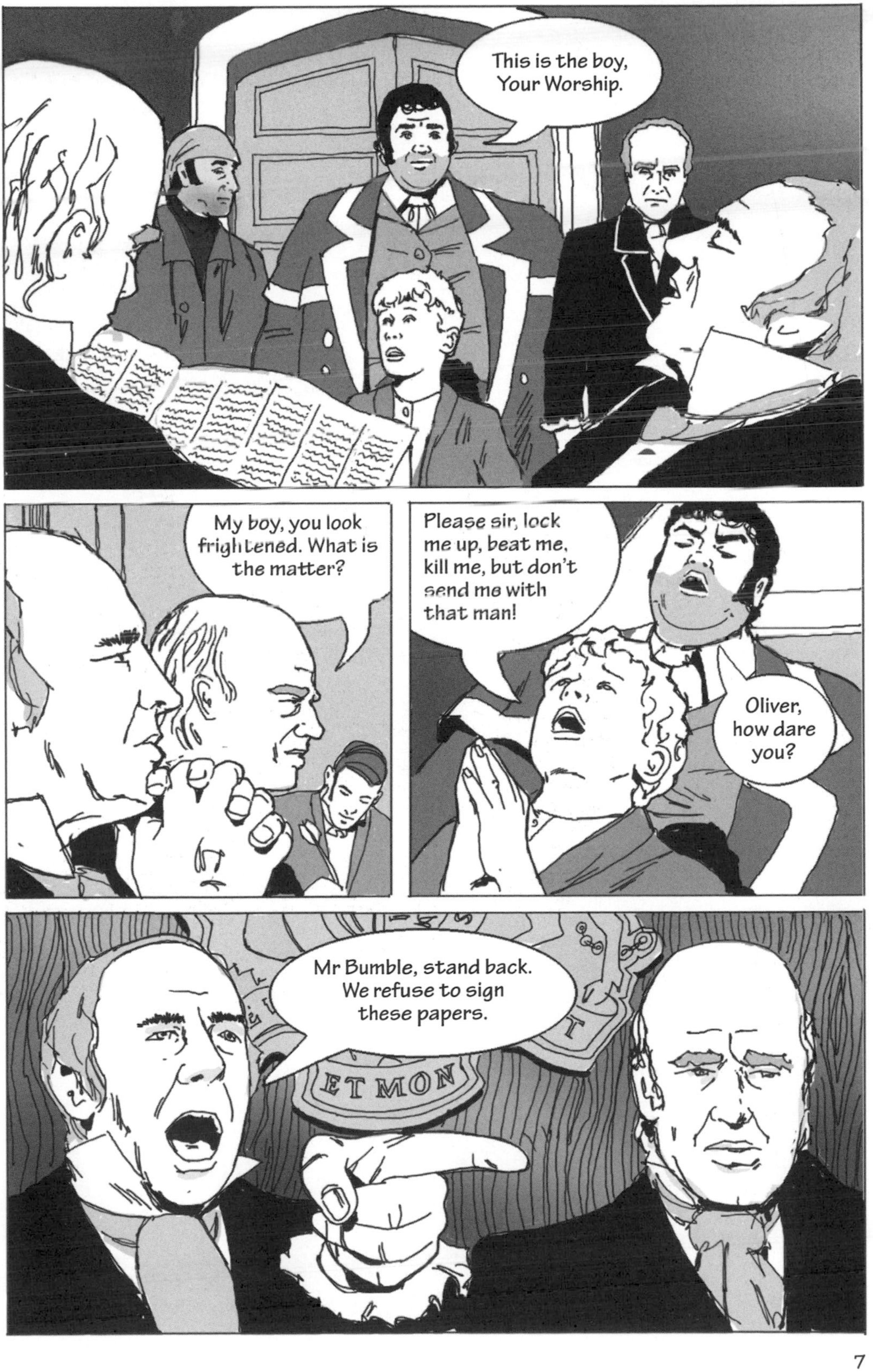
This is the boy, Your Worship.
My boy, you look frightened. What is the matter?
Please sir, lock me up, beat me, kill me, but don't send me with that man!
Oliver, how dare you?
Mr Bumble, stand back. We refuse to sign these papers.

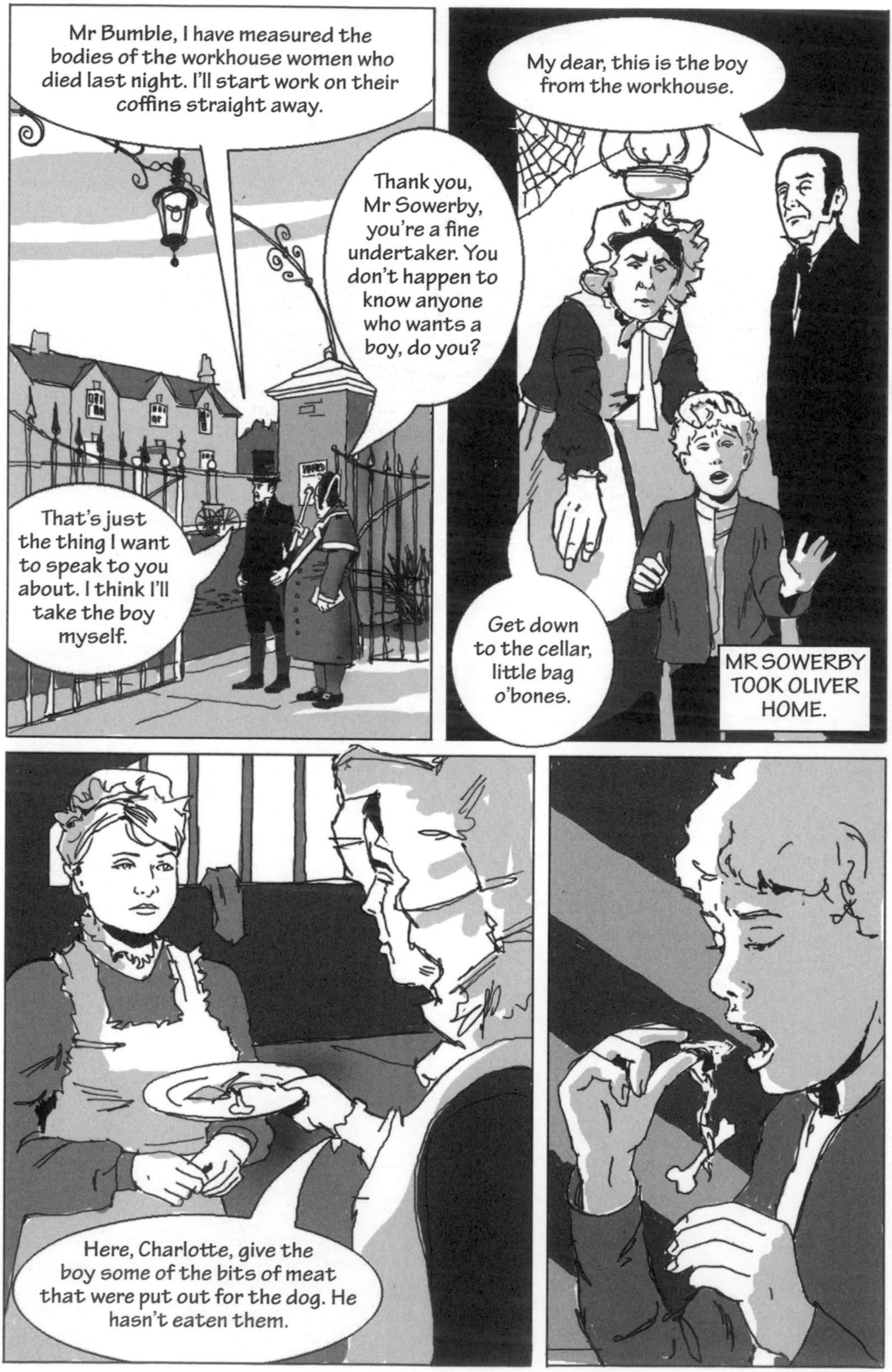
Mr Bumble, I have measured the bodies of the workhouse women who died last night. I'll start work on their coffins straight away.
Thank you, Mr Sowerby, you're a fine undertaker. You don't happen to know anyone who wants a boy, do you?
That's just the thing I want to speak to you about. I think I'll take the boy myself.
My dear, this is the boy from the workhouse.
Get down to the cellar, little bag o'bones.
MR SOWERBY TOOK OLIVER HOME.
Here, Charlotte, give the boy some of the bits of meat that were put out for the dog. He hasn't eaten them.

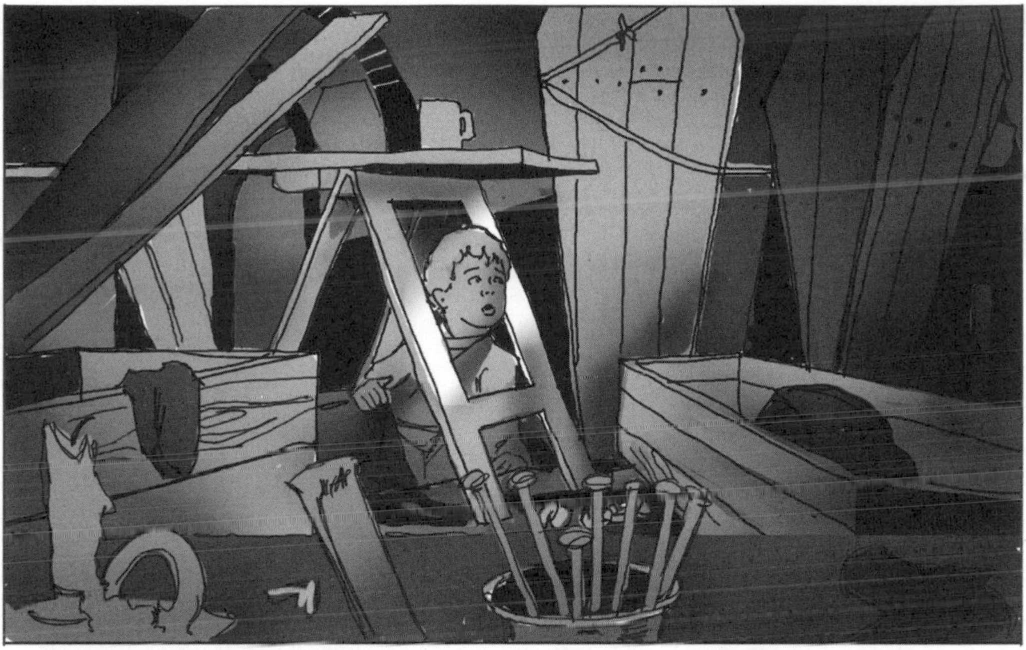

MR SOWERBY WAS AN UNDERTAKER. HE ARRANGED FUNERALS, HE MEASURED DEAD BODIES AND MADE COFFINS. OLIVER HAD TO SLEEP AMONG THE COFFINS.

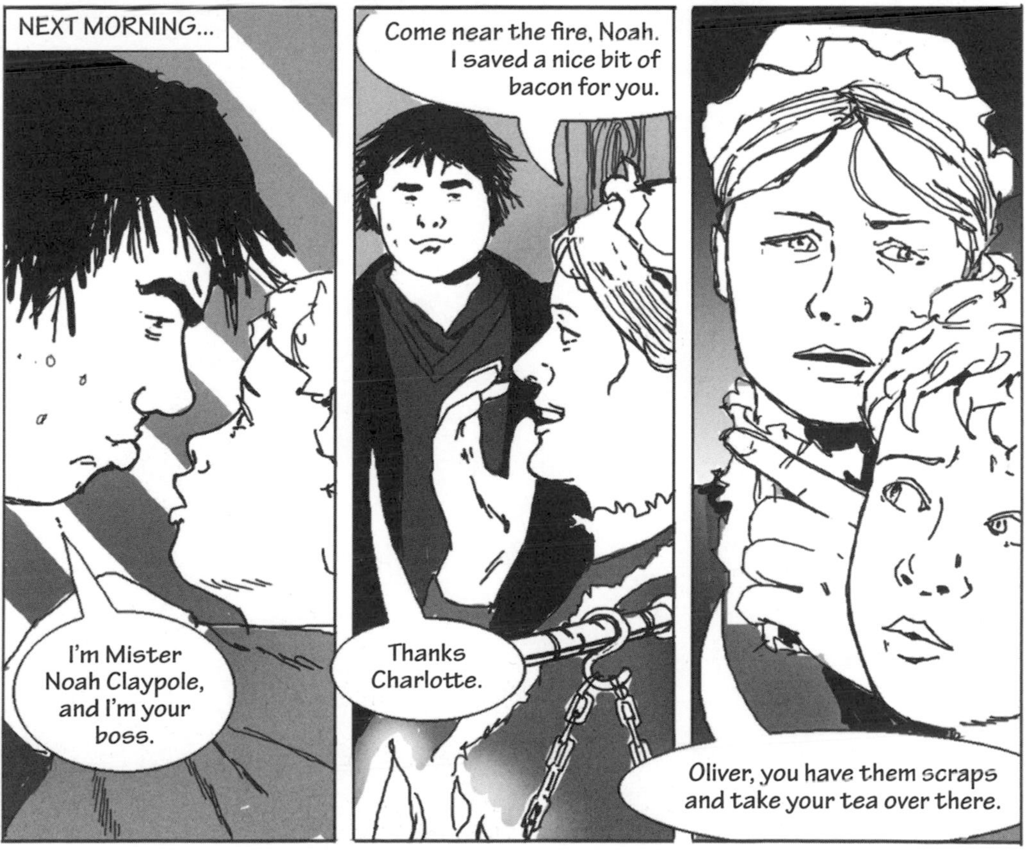
NEXT MORNING...
I'm Mister Noah Claypole, and I'm your boss.
Come near the fire, Noah. I saved a nice bit of bacon for you.
Thanks Charlotte.
Oliver, you have them scraps and take your tea over there.

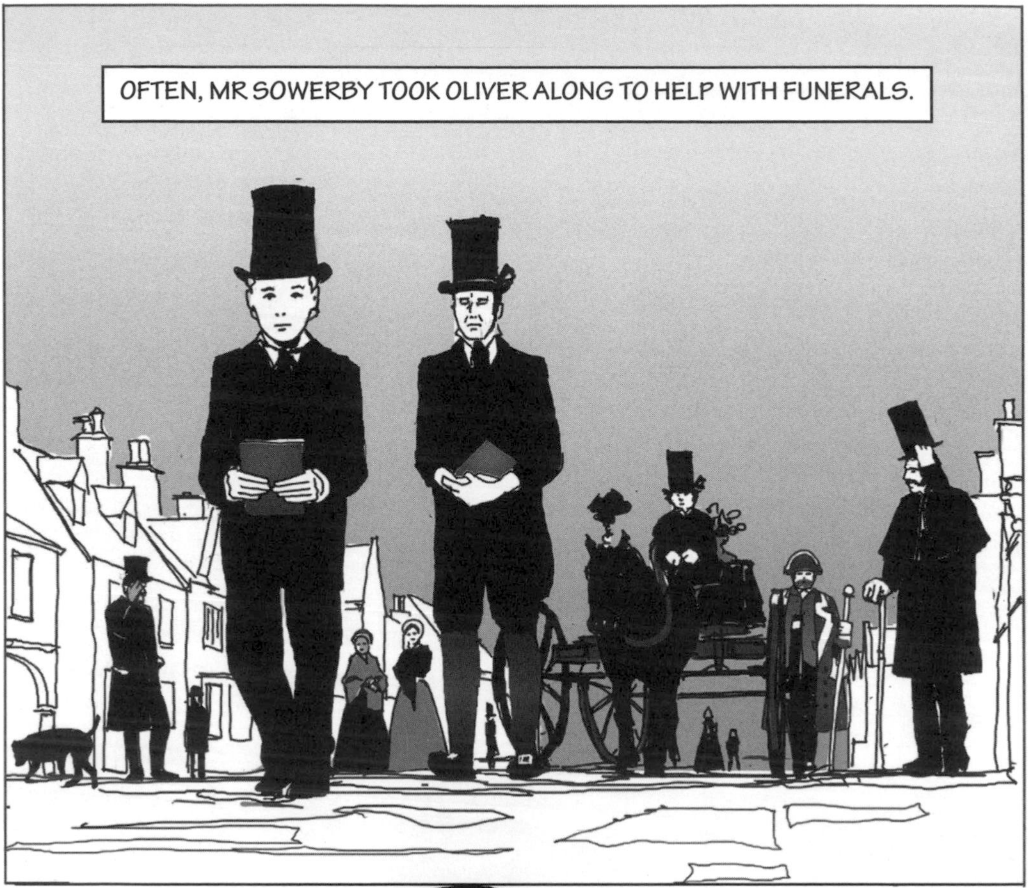
OFTEN, MR SOWERBY TOOK OLIVER ALONG TO HELP WITH FUNERALS.

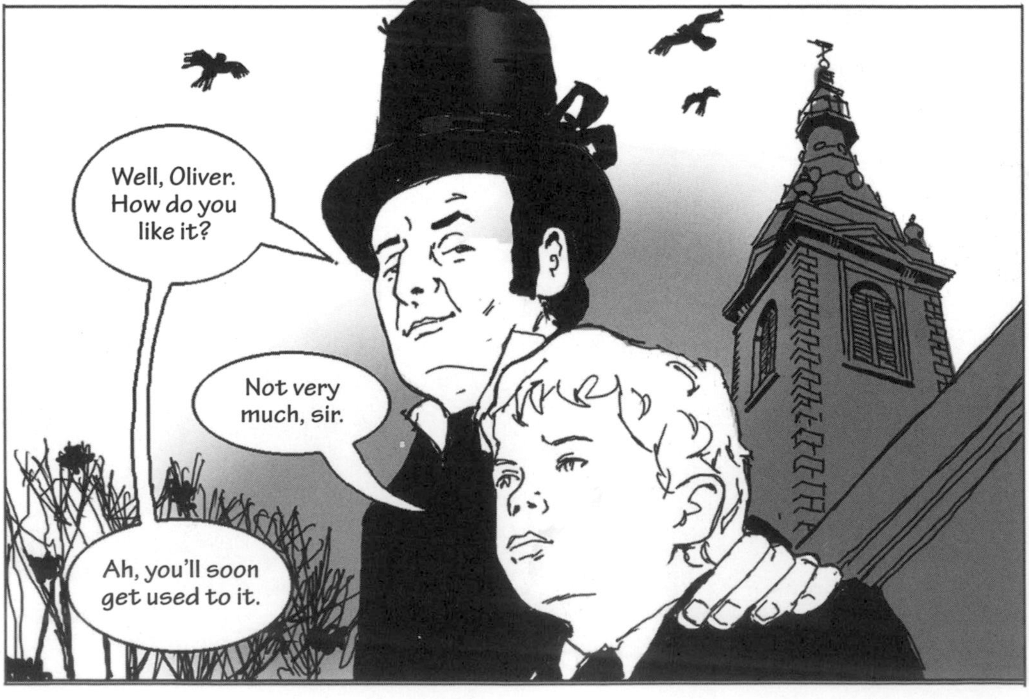
Well, Oliver. How do you like it?
Not very much, sir.
Ah, you'll soon get used to it.

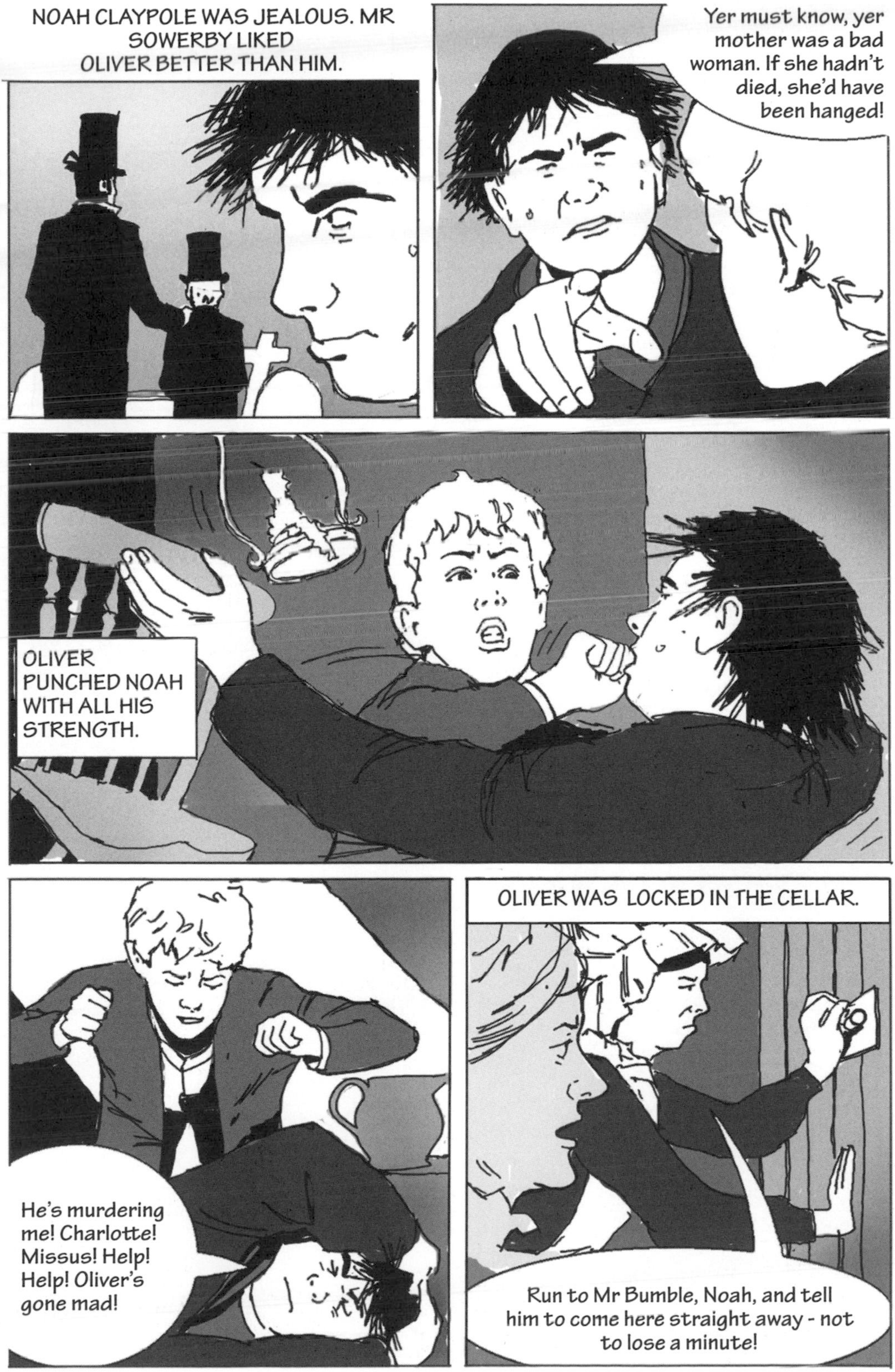
NOAH CLAYPOLE WAS JEALOUS. MR SOWERBY LIKED OLIVER BETTER THAN HIM.
Yer must know, yer mother was a bad woman. If she hadn't died, she'd have been hanged!
OLIVER PUNCHED NOAH WITH ALL HIS STRENGTH.
He's murdering me! Charlotte! Missus! Help! Help! Oliver's gone mad!
OLIVER WAS LOCKED IN THE CELLAR.
Run to Mr Bumble, Noah, and tell him to come here straight away - not to lose a minute!

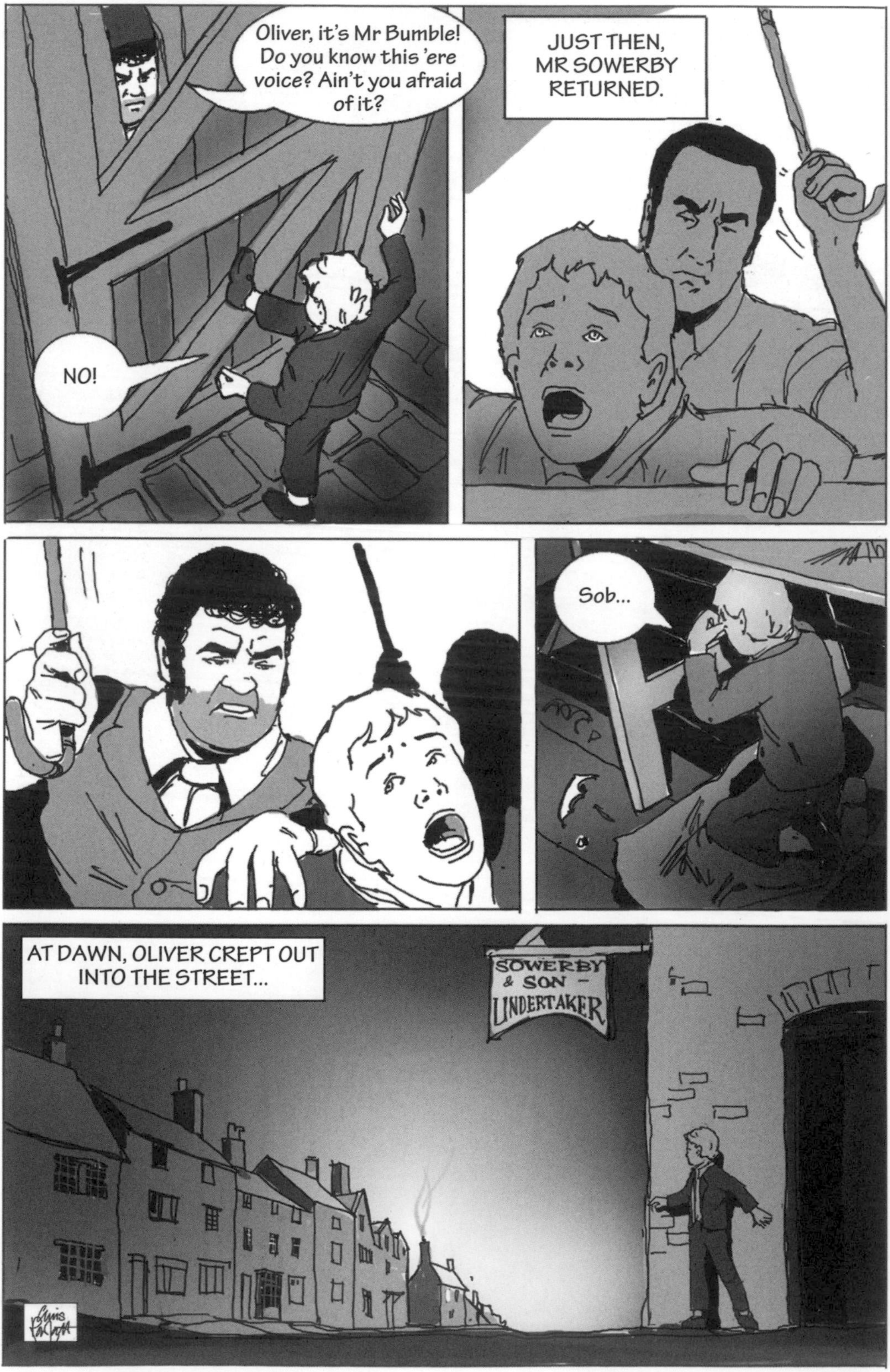
Oliver, it's Mr Bumble! Do you know this 'ere voice? Ain't you afraid of it?
NO!
JUST THEN, MR SOWERBY RETURNED.
Sob...
AT DAWN, OLIVER CREPT OUT INTO THE STREET...
SOWERBY & SON - UNDERTAKER

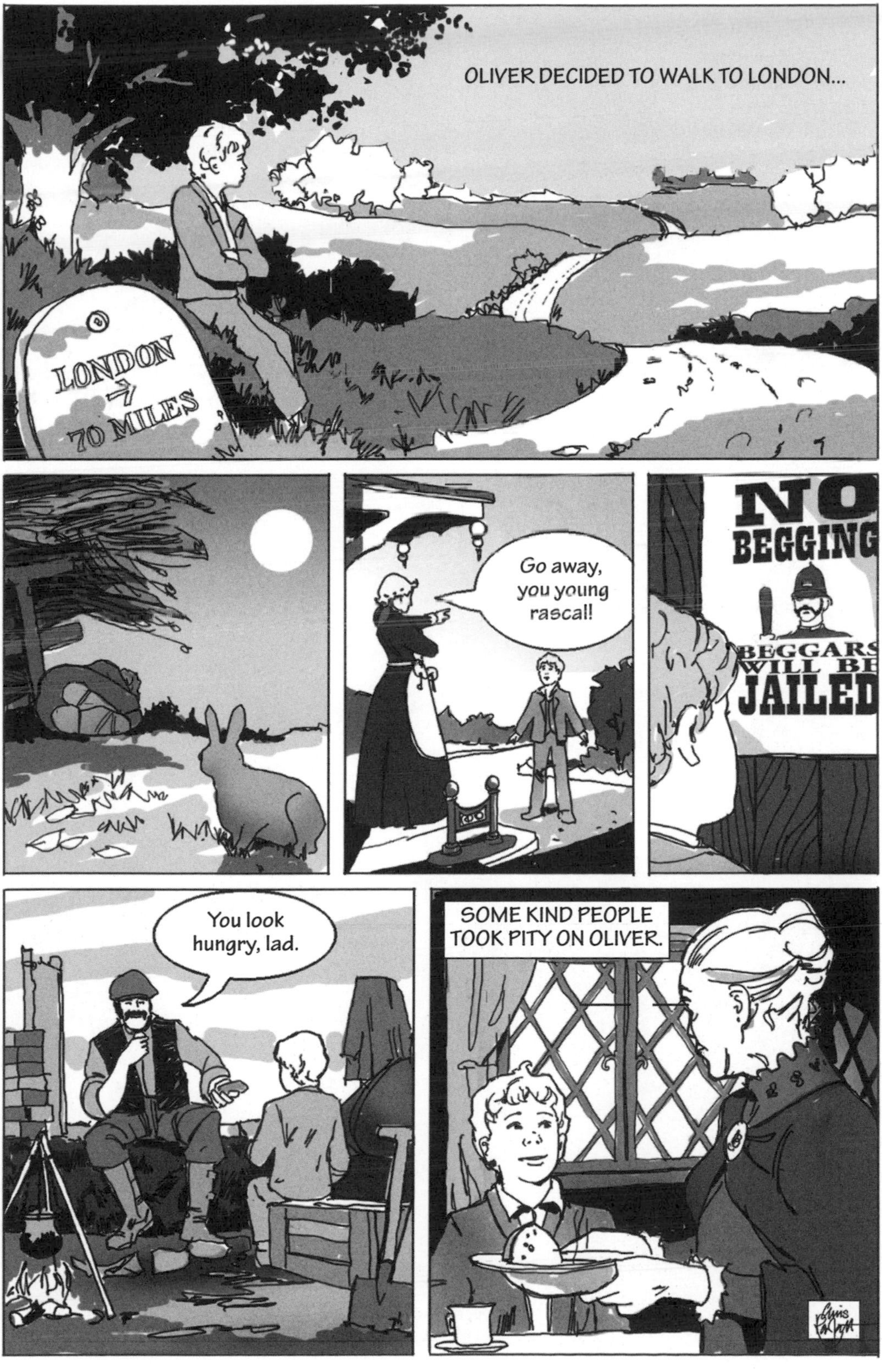
OLIVER DECIDED TO WALK TO LONDON...
LONDON
70 MILES
Go away, you young rascal!
NO
BEGGING
BEGGARS
WILL BE
JAILED
You look hungry, lad.
SOME KIND PEOPLE TOOK PITY ON OLIVER.

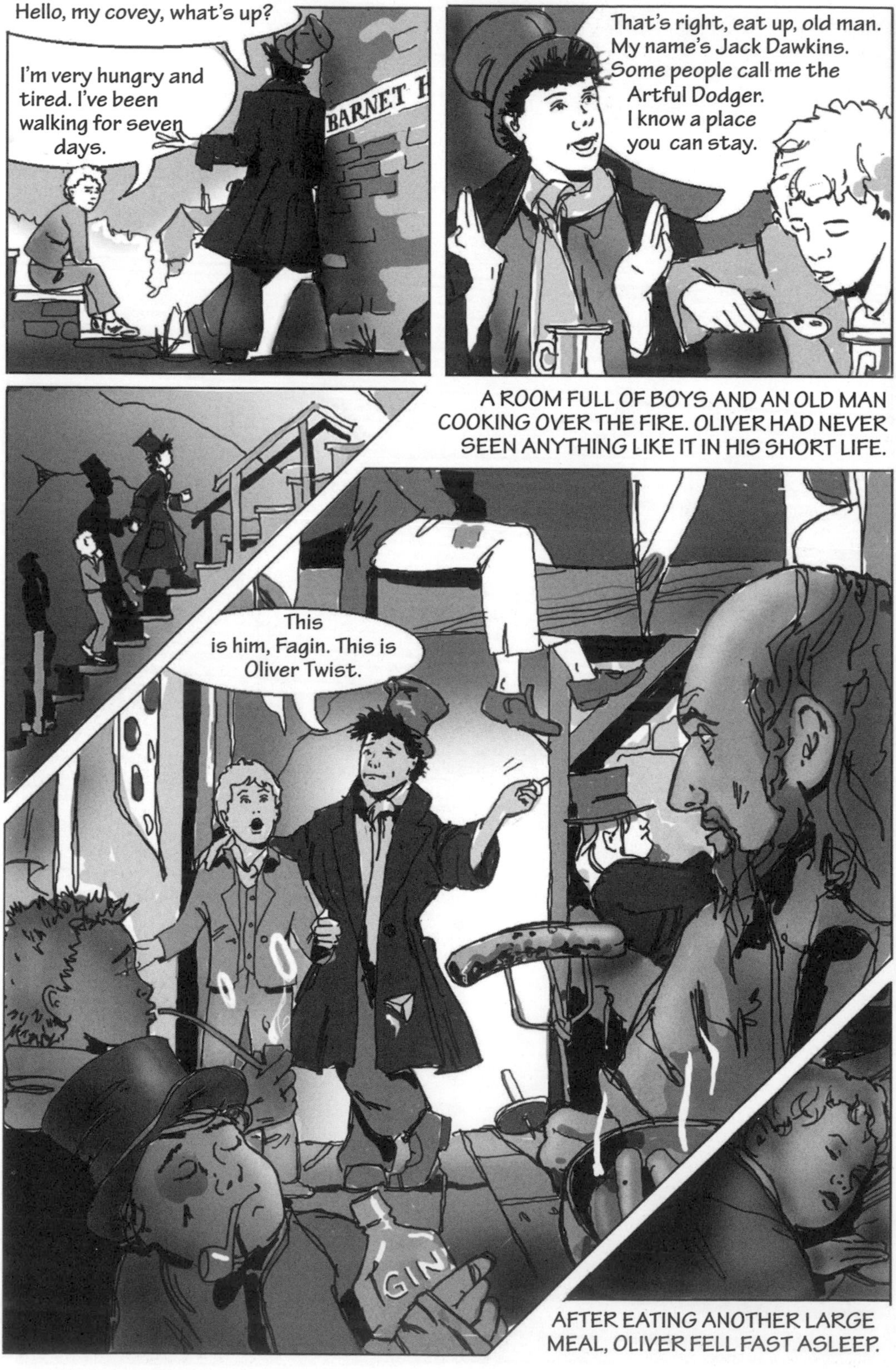

Hello, my covey, what's up?
I'm very hungry and tired. I've been walking for seven days.
BARNET H
That's right, eat up, old man. My name's Jack Dawkins. Some people call me the Artful Dodger. I know a place you can stay.
A ROOM FULL OF BOYS AND AN OLD MAN COOKING OVER THE FIRE. OLIVER HAD NEVER SEEN ANYTHING LIKE IT IN HIS SHORT LIFE.
This is him, Fagin. This is Oliver Twist.
GIN
AFTER EATING ANOTHER LARGE MEAL, OLIVER FELL FAST ASLEEP.

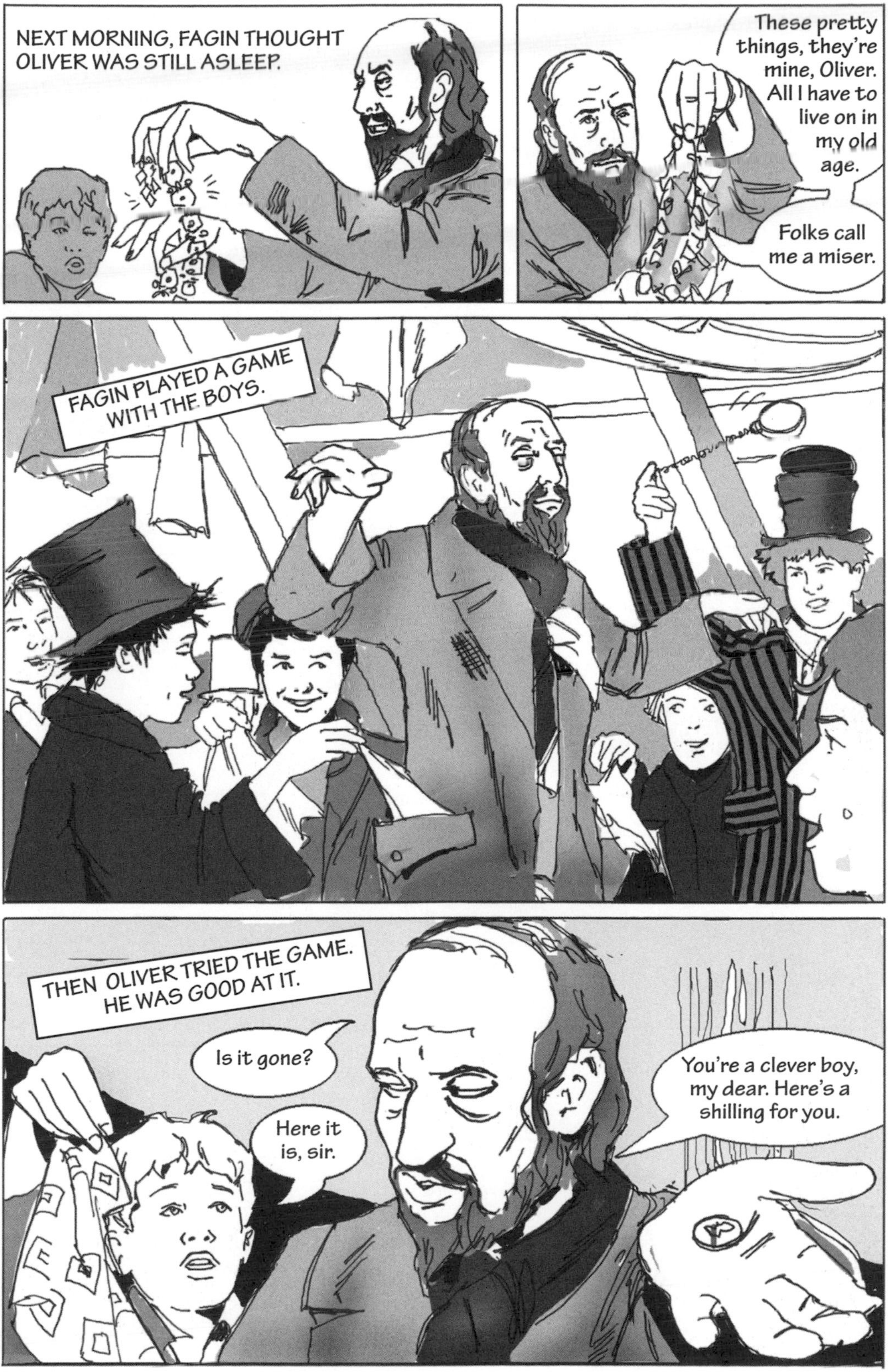
NEXT MORNING, FAGIN THOUGHT OLIVER WAS STILL ASLEEP.
These pretty things, they're mine, Oliver. All I have to live on in my old age.
Folks call me a miser.
FAGIN PLAYED A GAME WITH THE BOYS.
THEN OLIVER TRIED THE GAME. HE WAS GOOD AT IT.
Is it gone?
Here it is, sir.
You're a clever boy, my dear. Here's a shilling for you.

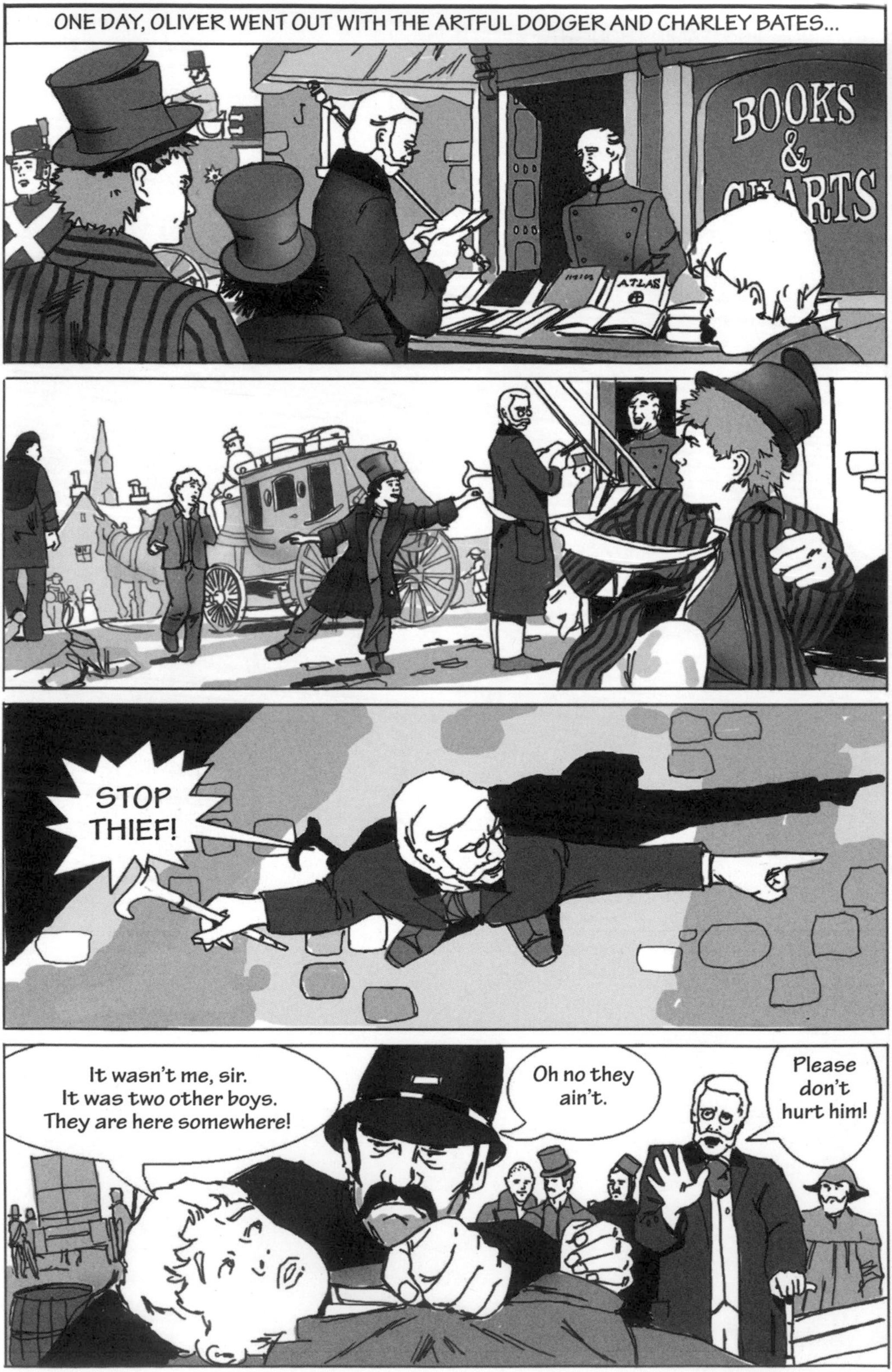
ONE DAY, OLIVER WENT OUT WITH THE ARTFUL DODGER AND CHARLEY BATES...
BOOKS & CHARTS
ATLAS
STOP THIEF!
It wasn't me, sir. It was two other boys. They are here somewhere!
Oh no they ain't.
Please don't hurt him!

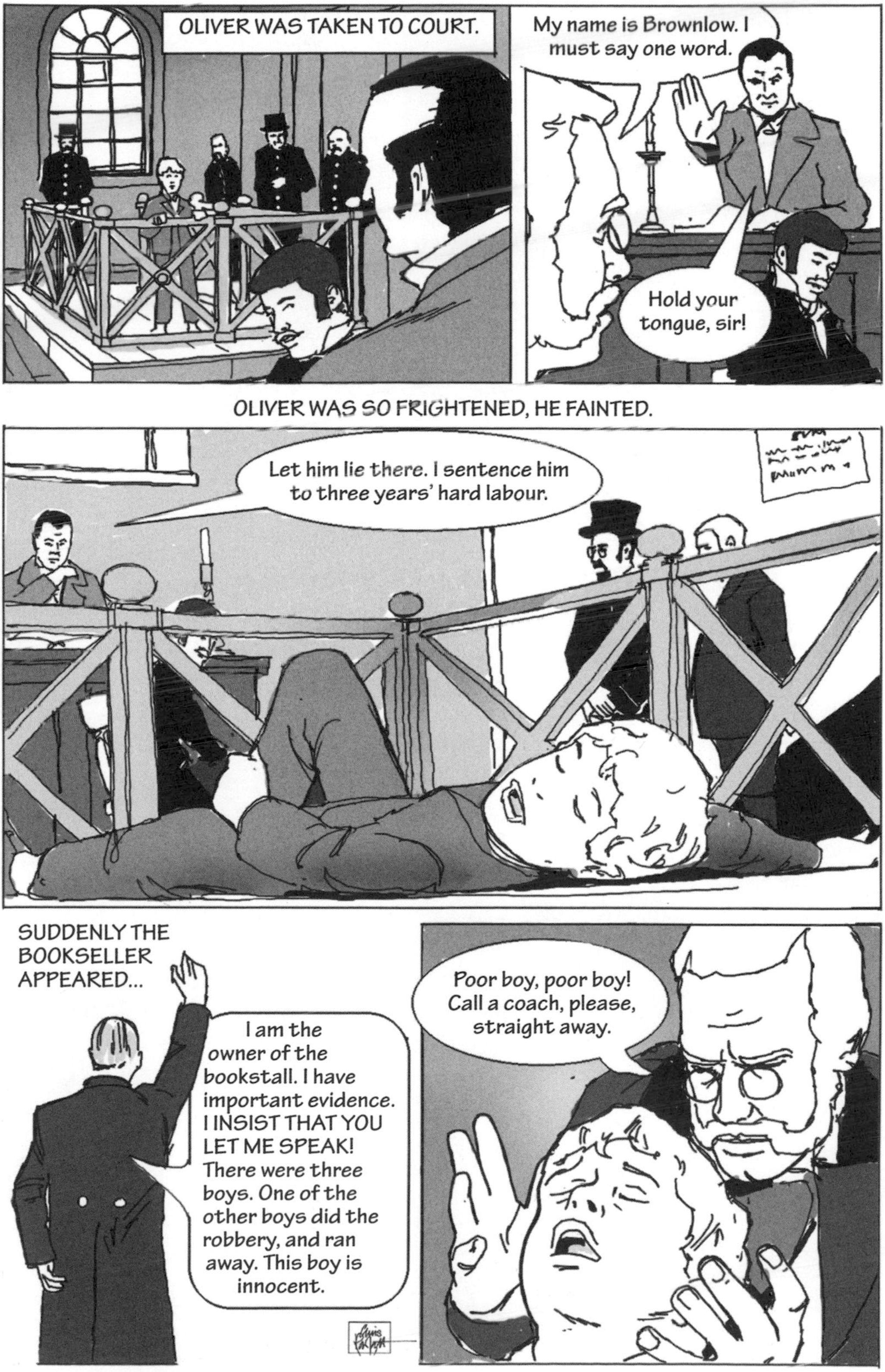
OLIVER WAS TAKEN TO COURT.
My name is Brownlow. I must say one word.
Hold your tongue, sir!
OLIVER WAS SO FRIGHTENED, HE FAINTED.
Let him lie there. I sentence him to three years' hard labour.
SUDDENLY THE BOOKSELLER APPEARED...
I am the owner of the bookstall. I have important evidence. I INSIST THAT YOU LET ME SPEAK! There were three boys. One of the other boys did the robbery, and ran away. This boy is innocent.
Poor boy, poor boy! Call a coach, please, straight away.

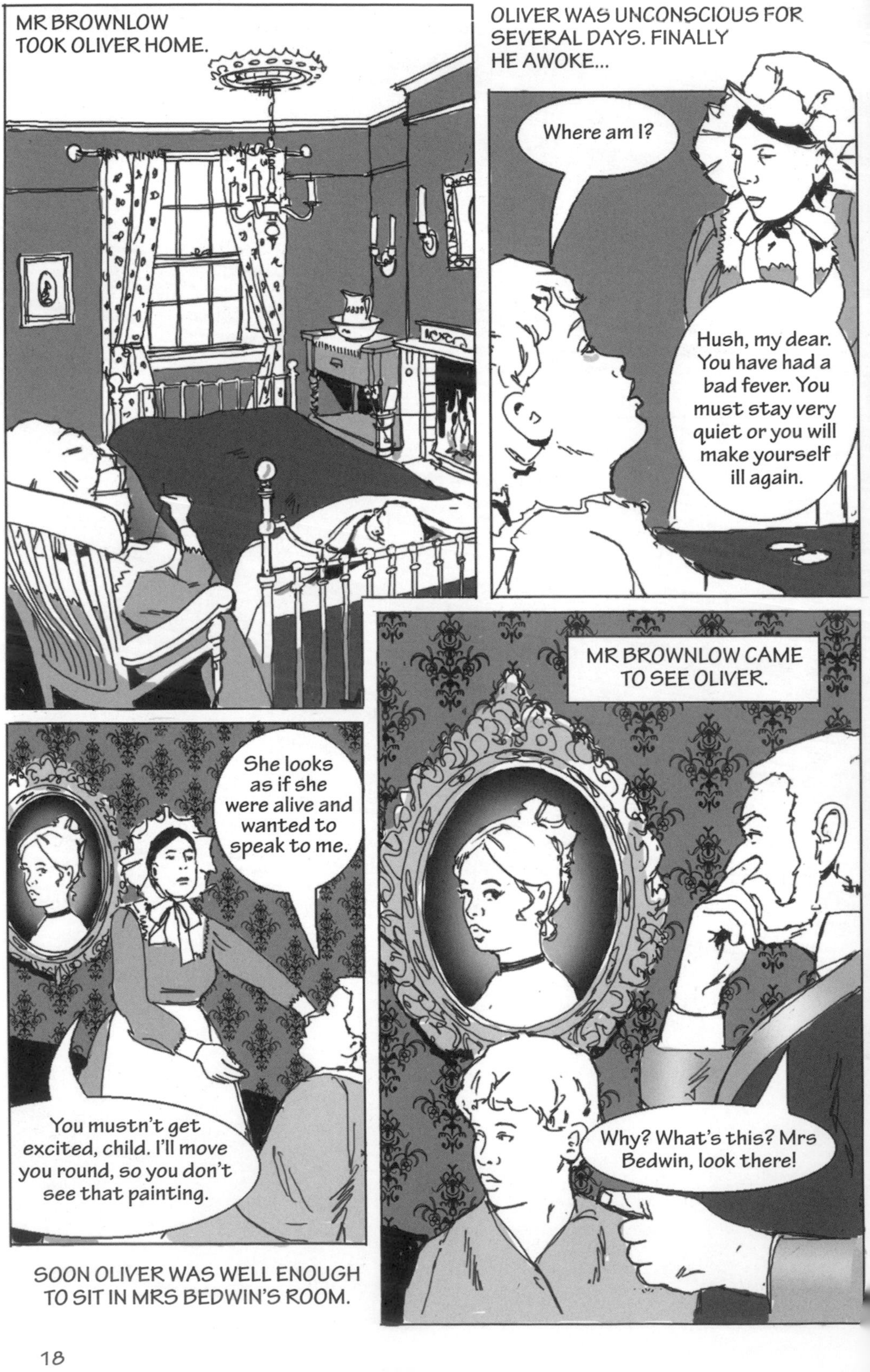
MR BROWNLOW TOOK OLIVER HOME.
OLIVER WAS UNCONSCIOUS FOR SEVERAL DAYS. FINALLY HE AWOKE...
Where am I?
Hush, my dear. You have had a bad fever. You must stay very quiet or you will make yourself ill again.
SOON OLIVER WAS WELL ENOUGH TO SIT IN MRS BEDWIN'S ROOM.
She looks as if she were alive and wanted to speak to me.
You mustn't get excited, child. I'll move you round, so you don't see that painting.
MR BROWNLOW CAME TO SEE OLIVER.
Why? What's this? Mrs Bedwin, look there!

AFTER THE ROBBERY, THE ARTFUL DODGER AND CHARLEY BATES ESCAPED AND GOT BACK TO FAGIN'S.

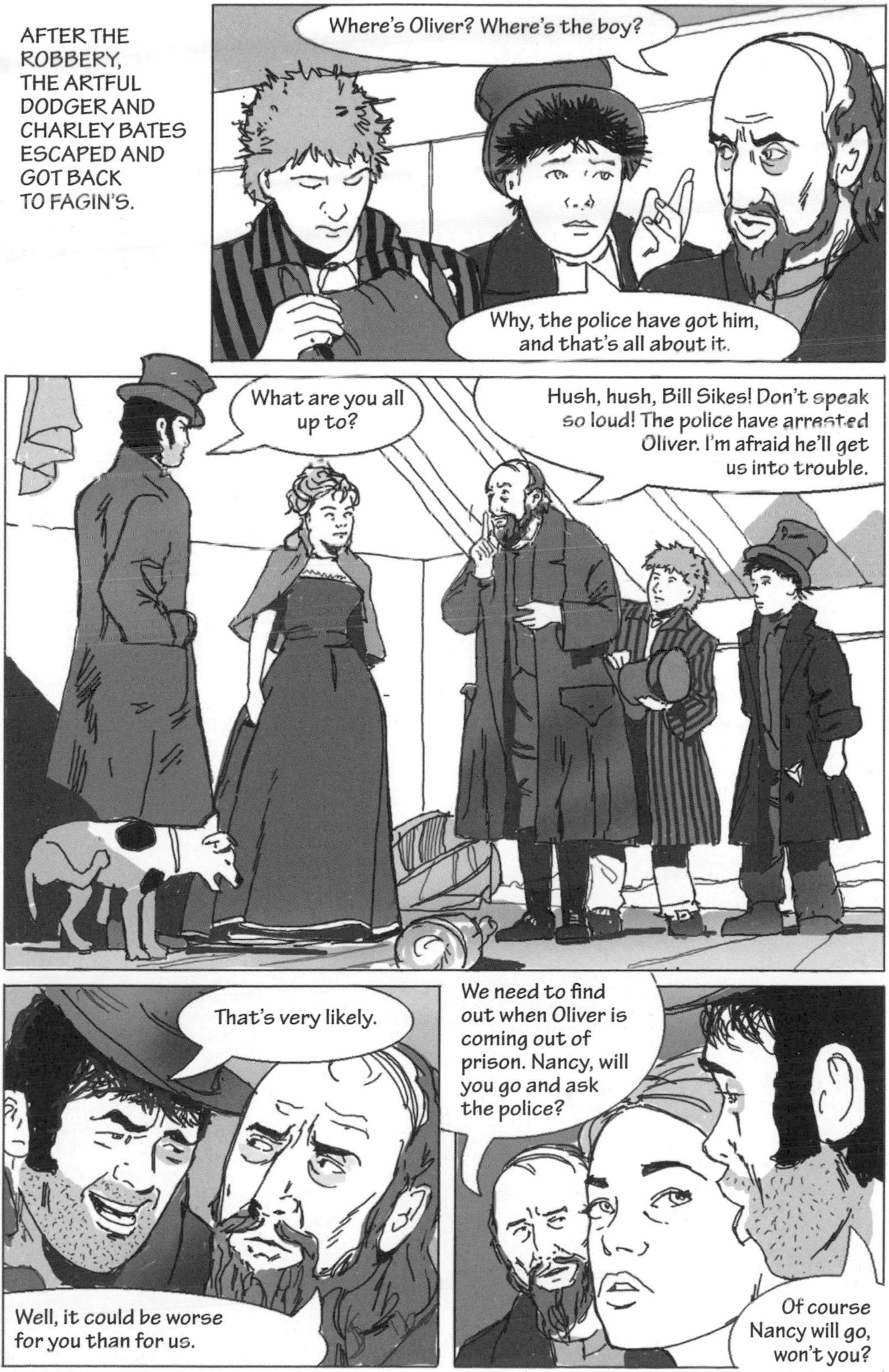

Where's Oliver? Where's the boy?
Why, the police have got him, and that's all about it.
What are you all up to?
Hush, hush, Bill Sikes! Don't speak so loud! The police have arrested Oliver. I'm afraid he'll get us into trouble.
That's very likely.
Well, it could be worse for you than for us.
We need to find out when Oliver is coming out of prison. Nancy, will you go and ask the police?
Of course Nancy will go, won't you?

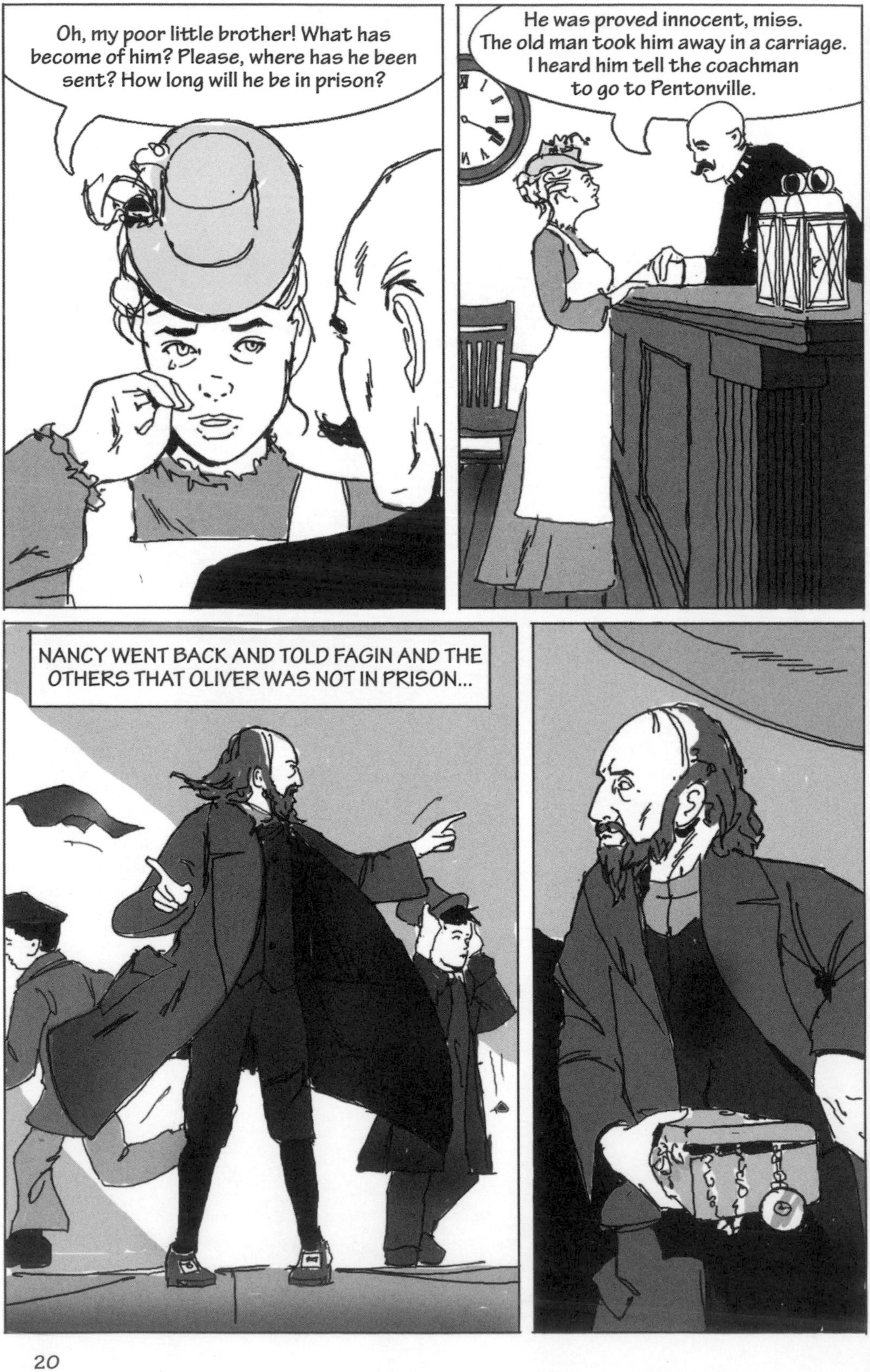
Oh, my poor little brother! What has become of him? Please, where has he been sent? How long will he be in prison?
He was proved innocent, miss. The old man took him away in a carriage. I heard him tell the coachman to go to Pentonville.
NANCY WENT BACK AND TOLD FAGIN AND THE OTHERS THAT OLIVER WAS NOT IN PRISON...

AT MR BROWNLOW'S HOUSE, EVERYTHING WAS QUIET AND NEAT. EVERYONE WAS KIND AND GENTLE TO OLIVER. AFTER HIS HARD LIFE IT SEEMED LIKE HEAVEN.

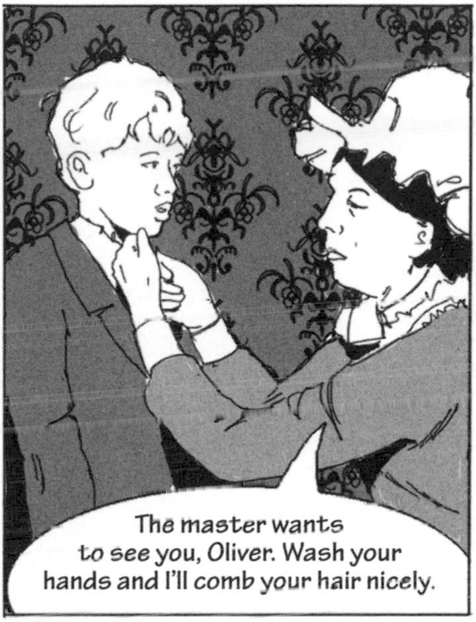
The master wants to see you, Oliver. Wash your hands and I'll comb your hair nicely.

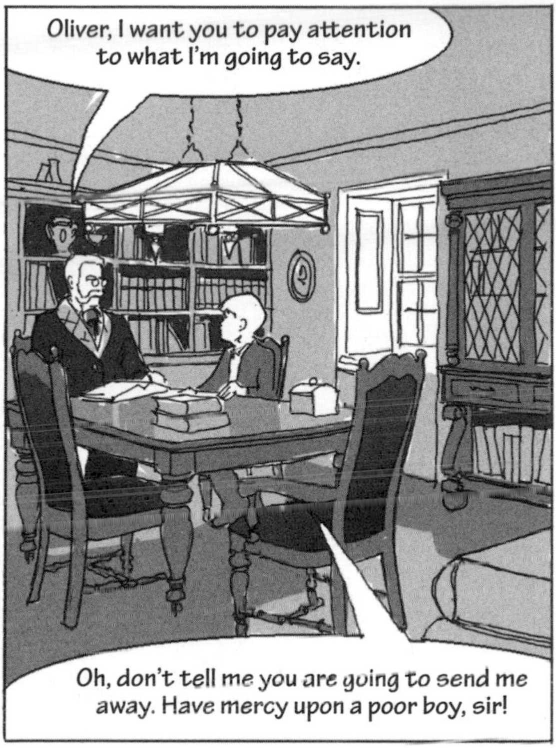
Oliver, I want you to pay attention to what I'm going to say.
Oh, don't tell me you are going to send me away. Have mercy upon a poor boy, sir!

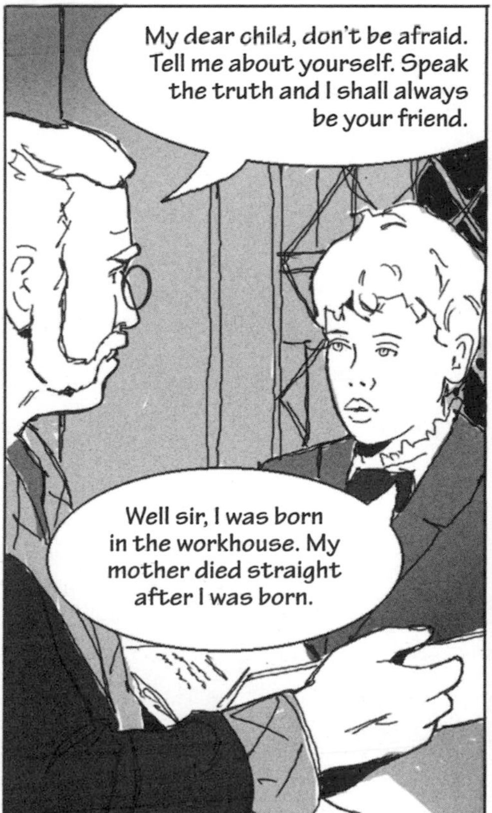
My dear child, don't be afraid. Tell me about yourself. Speak the truth and I shall always be your friend.
Well sir, I was born in the workhouse. My mother died straight after I was born.

SUDDENLY THEY WERE INTERRUPTED. MR BROWNLOW'S FRIEND, MR GRIMWIG, HAD COME TO TEA.

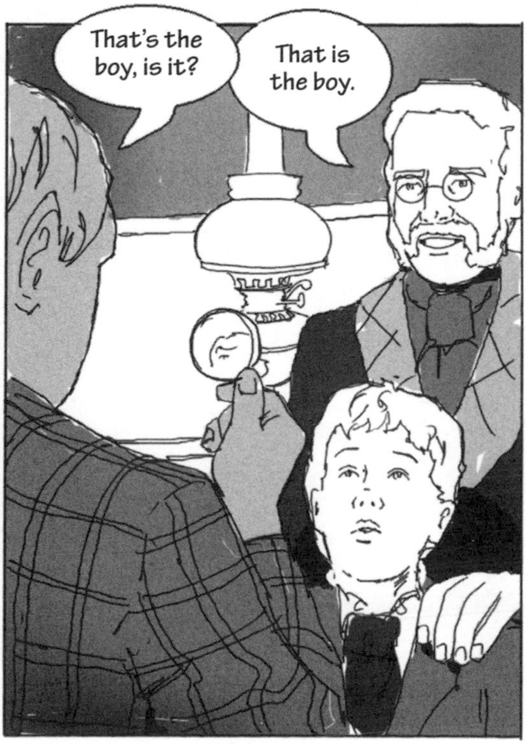
That's the boy, is it?
That is the boy.

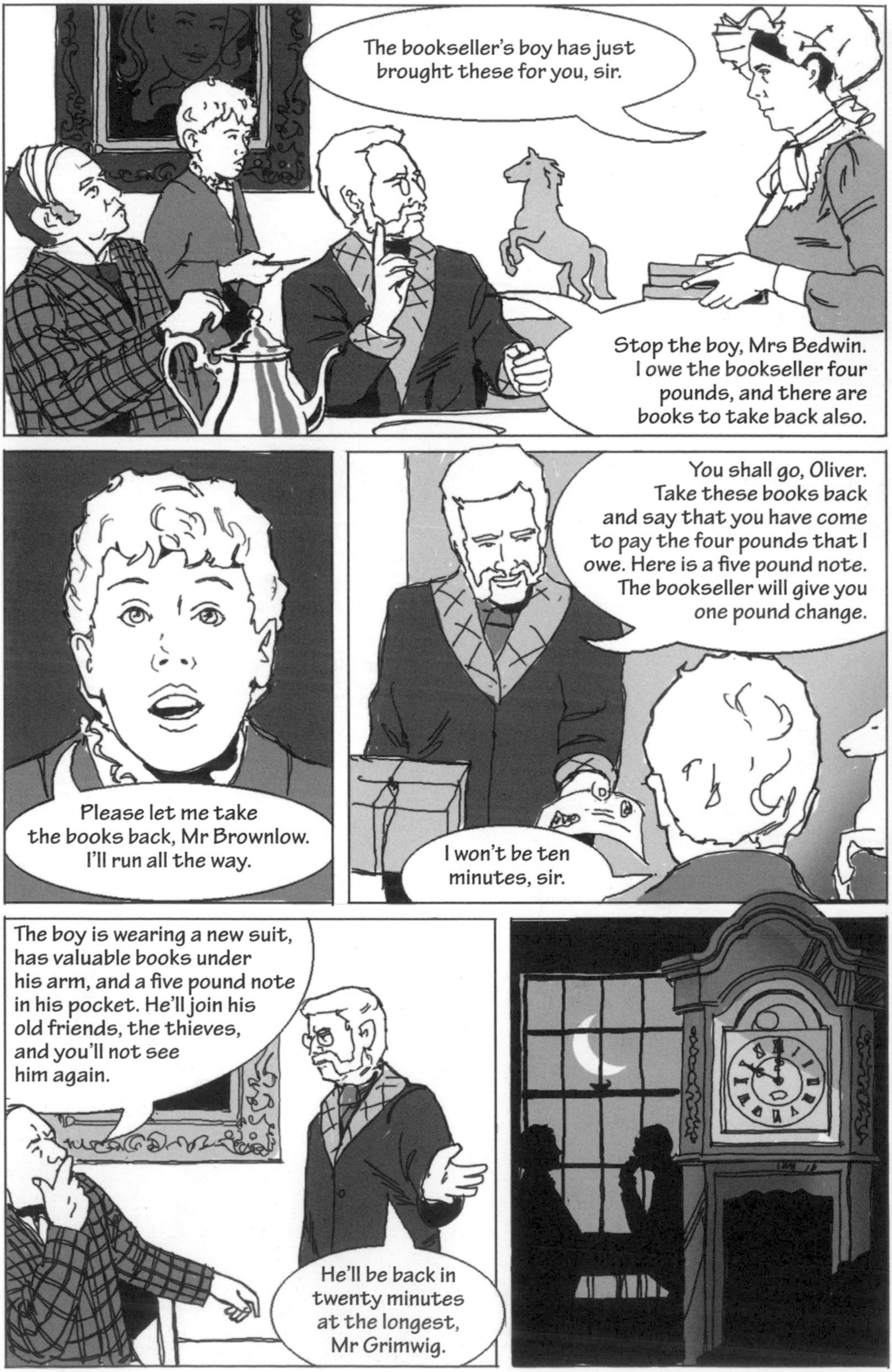
The bookseller's boy has just brought these for you, sir.
Stop the boy, Mrs Bedwin. I owe the bookseller four pounds, and there are books to take back also.
Please let me take the books back, Mr Brownlow. I'll run all the way.
You shall go, Oliver. Take these books back and say that you have come to pay the four pounds that I owe. Here is a five pound note. The bookseller will give you one pound change.
I won't be ten minutes, sir.
The boy is wearing a new suit, has valuable books under his arm, and a five pound note in his pocket. He'll join his old friends, the thieves, and you'll not see him again.
He'll be back in twenty minutes at the longest, Mr Grimwig.

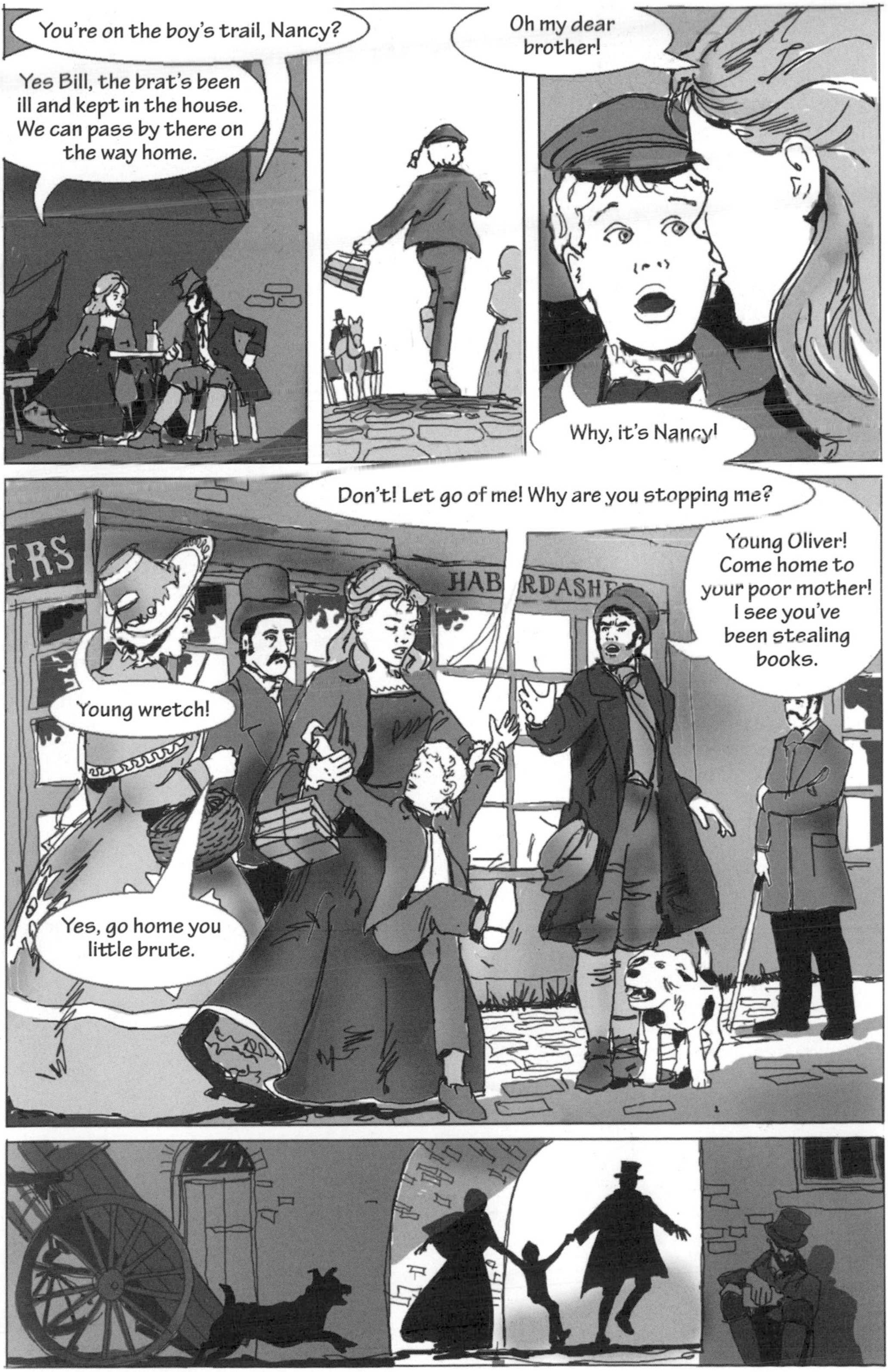
You're on the boy's trail, Nancy?
Yes Bill, the brat's been ill and kept in the house. We can pass by there on the way home.
Oh my dear brother!
Why, it's Nancy!
Don't! Let go of me! Why are you stopping me?
Young Oliver! Come home to your poor mother! I see you've been stealing books.
Young wretch!
Yes, go home you little brute.
HABERDASHE

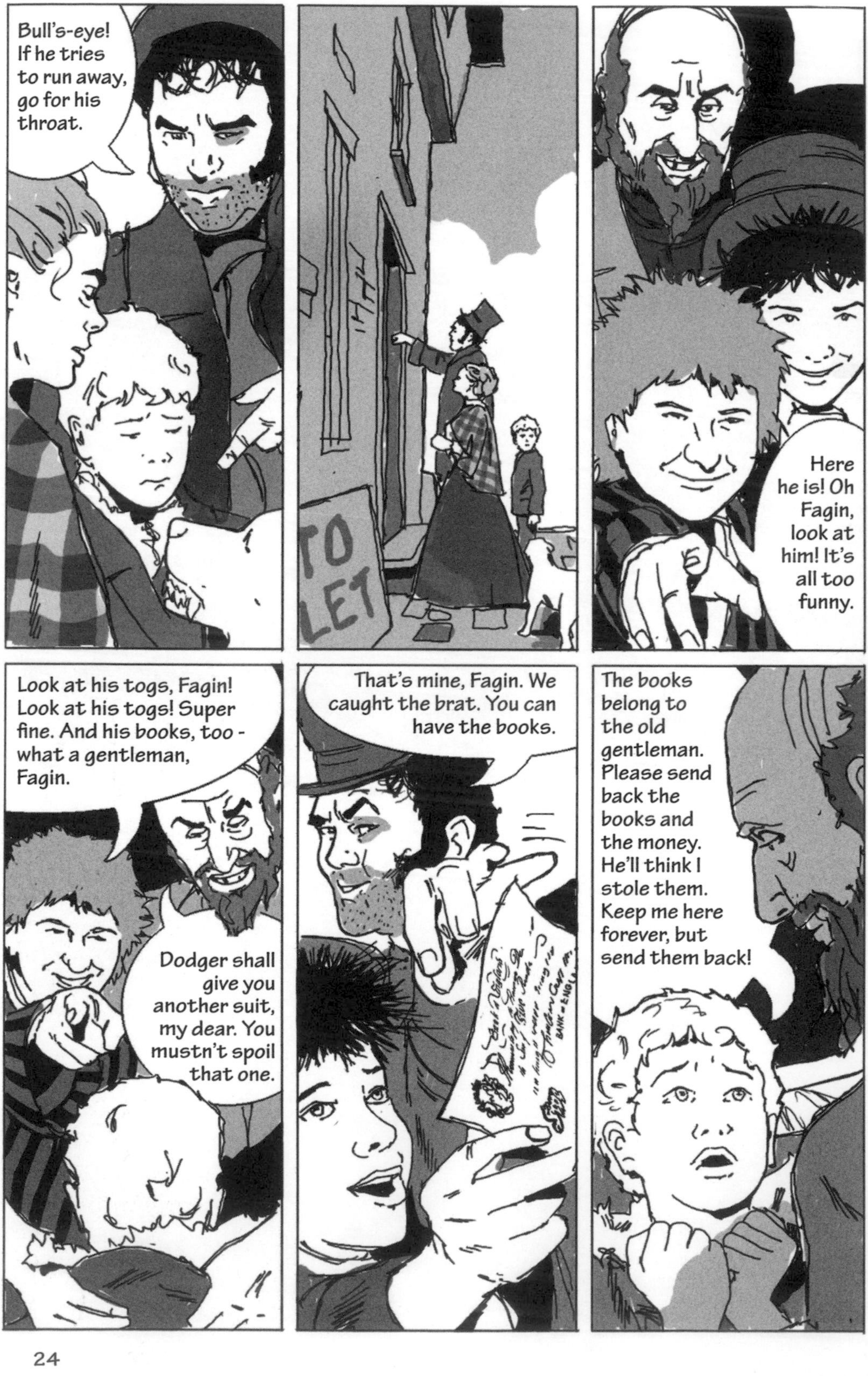

Bull's-eye! If he tries to run away, go for his throat.
TO LET
Here he is! Oh Fagin, look at him! It's all too funny.
Look at his togs, Fagin! Look at his togs! Super fine. And his books, too - what a gentleman, Fagin.
Dodger shall give you another suit, my dear. You mustn't spoil that one.
That's mine, Fagin. We caught the brat. You can have the books.
The books belong to the old gentleman. Please send back the books and the money. He'll think I stole them. Keep me here forever, but send them back!

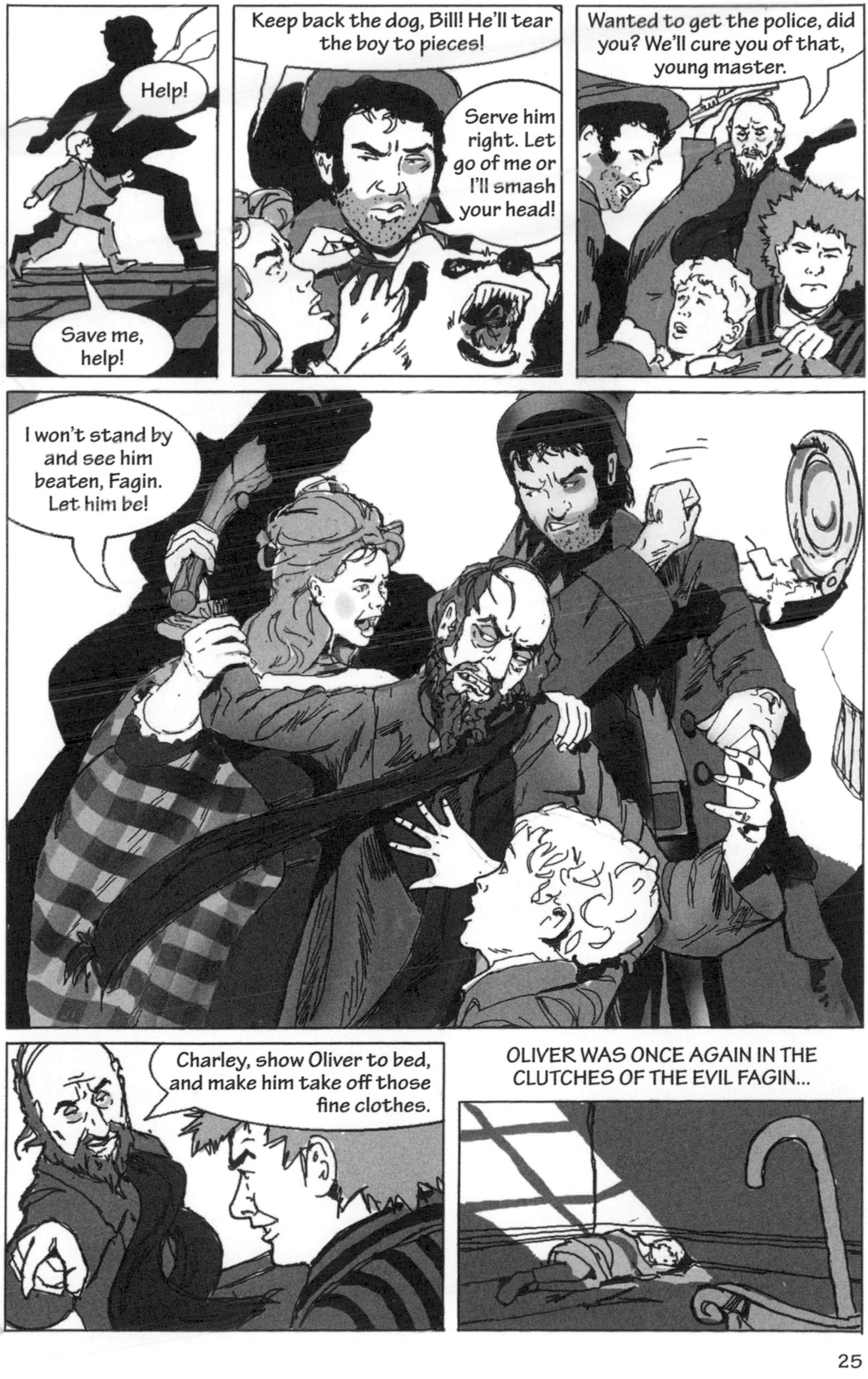
Help!
Save me, help!
Keep back the dog, Bill! He'll tear the boy to pieces!
Serve him right. Let go of me or I'll smash your head!
Wanted to get the police, did you? We'll cure you of that, young master.
I won't stand by and see him beaten, Fagin. Let him be!
Charley, show Oliver to bed, and make him take off those fine clothes.
OLIVER WAS ONCE AGAIN IN THE CLUTCHES OF THE EVIL FAGIN...

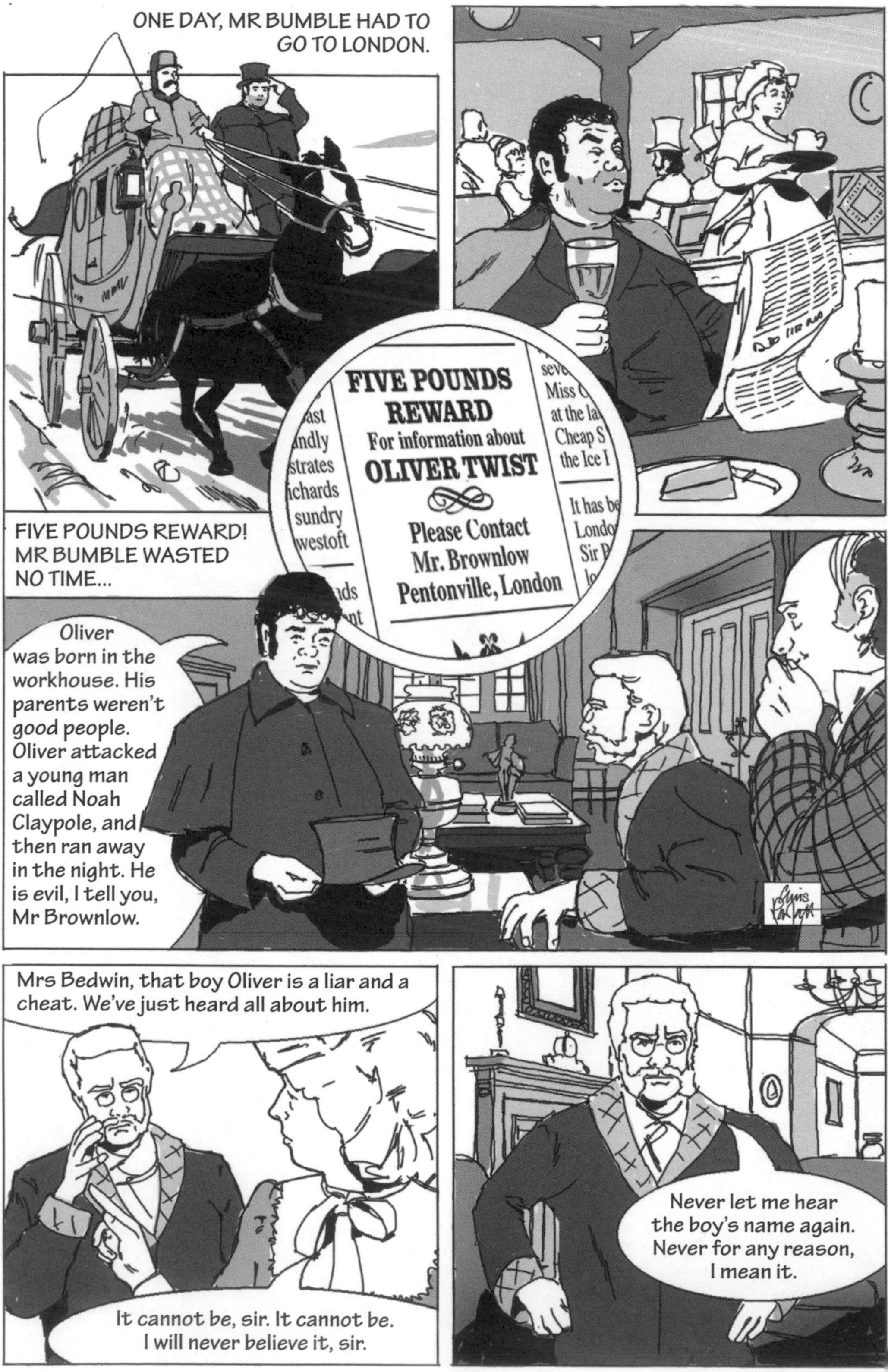
ONE DAY, MR BUMBLE HAD TO GO TO LONDON.
FIVE POUNDS REWARD
For information about
OLIVER TWIST
Please Contact
Mr. Brownlow
Pentonville, London
FIVE POUNDS REWARD! MR BUMBLE WASTED NO TIME...
Oliver was born in the workhouse. His parents weren't good people. Oliver attacked a young man called Noah Claypole, and then ran away in the night. He is evil, I tell you, Mr Brownlow.
Mrs Bedwin, that boy Oliver is a liar and a cheat. We've just heard all about him.
It cannot be, sir. It cannot be. I will never believe it, sir.
Never let me hear the boy's name again. Never for any reason, I mean it.

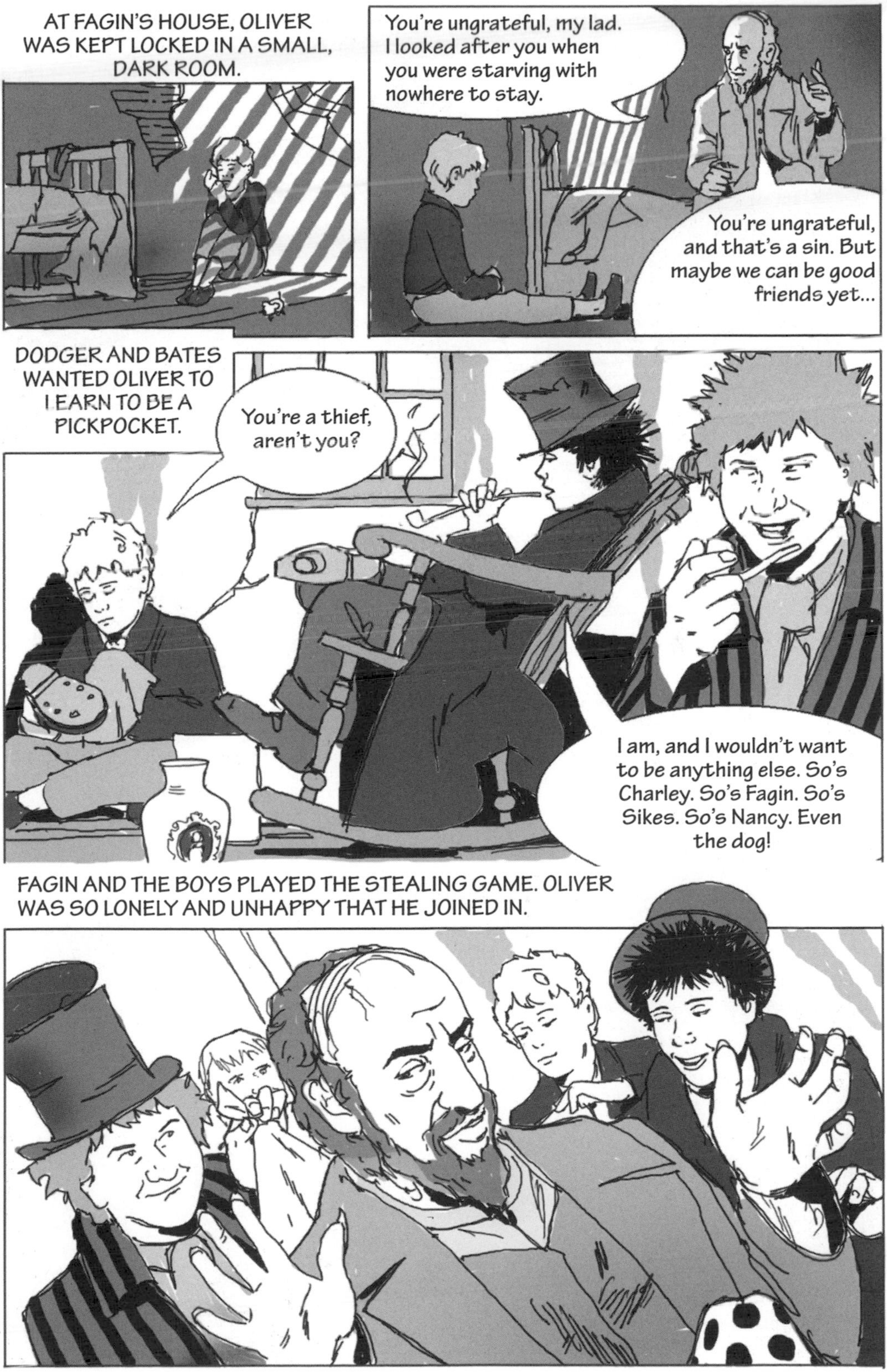
AT FAGIN'S HOUSE, OLIVER WAS KEPT LOCKED IN A SMALL, DARK ROOM.
You're ungrateful, my lad. I looked after you when you were starving with nowhere to stay.
You're ungrateful, and that's a sin. But maybe we can be good friends yet...
DODGER AND BATES WANTED OLIVER TO LEARN TO BE A PICKPOCKET.
You're a thief, aren't you?
I am, and I wouldn't want to be anything else. So's Charley. So's Fagin. So's Sikes. So's Nancy. Even the dog!
FAGIN AND THE BOYS PLAYED THE STEALING GAME. OLIVER WAS SO LONELY AND UNHAPPY THAT HE JOINED IN.

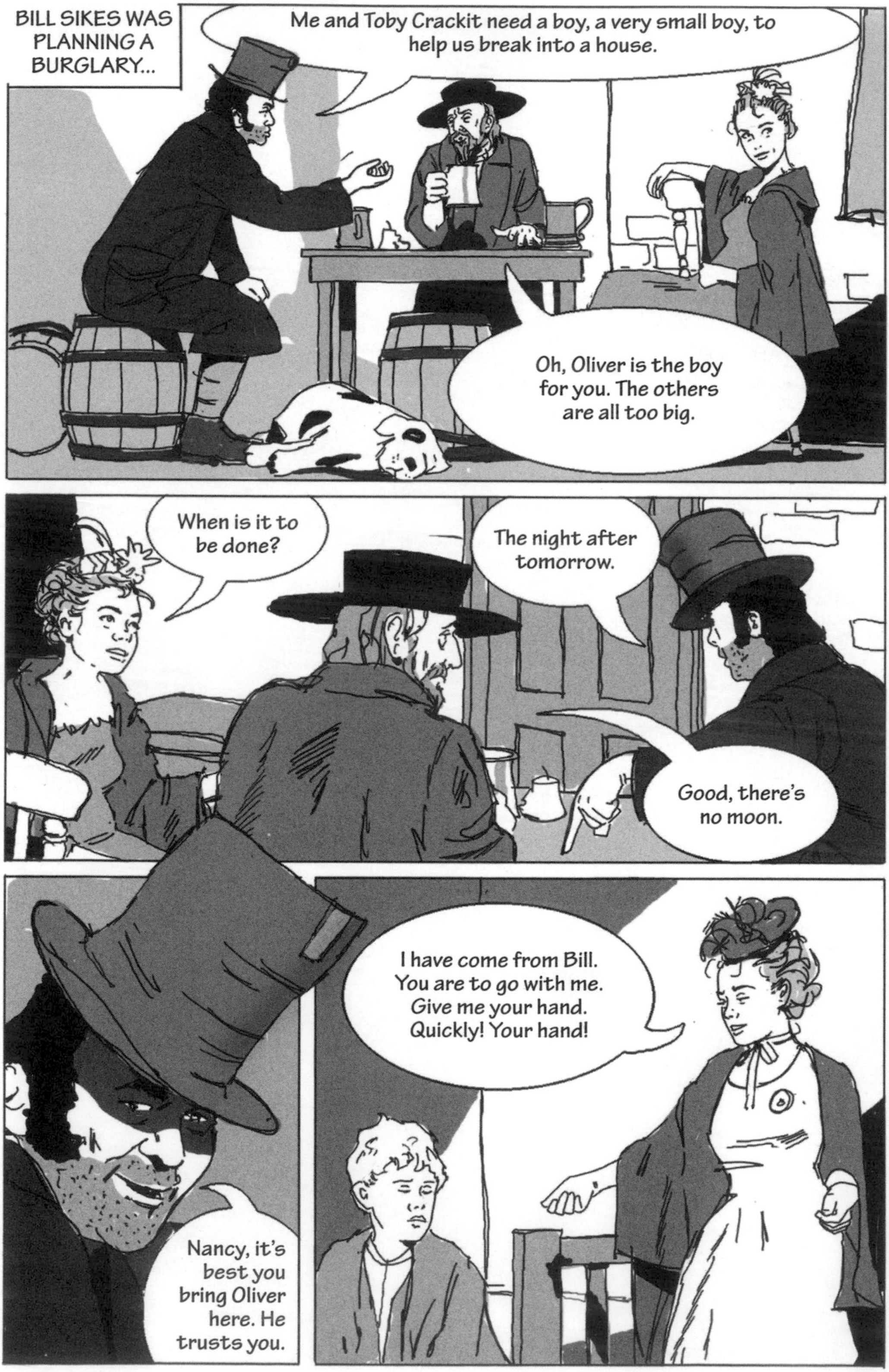
BILL SIKES WAS PLANNING A BURGLARY...
Me and Toby Crackit need a boy, a very small boy, to help us break into a house.
Oh, Oliver is the boy for you. The others are all too big.
When is it to be done?
The night after tomorrow.
Good, there's no moon.
Nancy, it's best you bring Oliver here. He trusts you.
I have come from Bill. You are to go with me. Give me your hand. Quickly! Your hand!

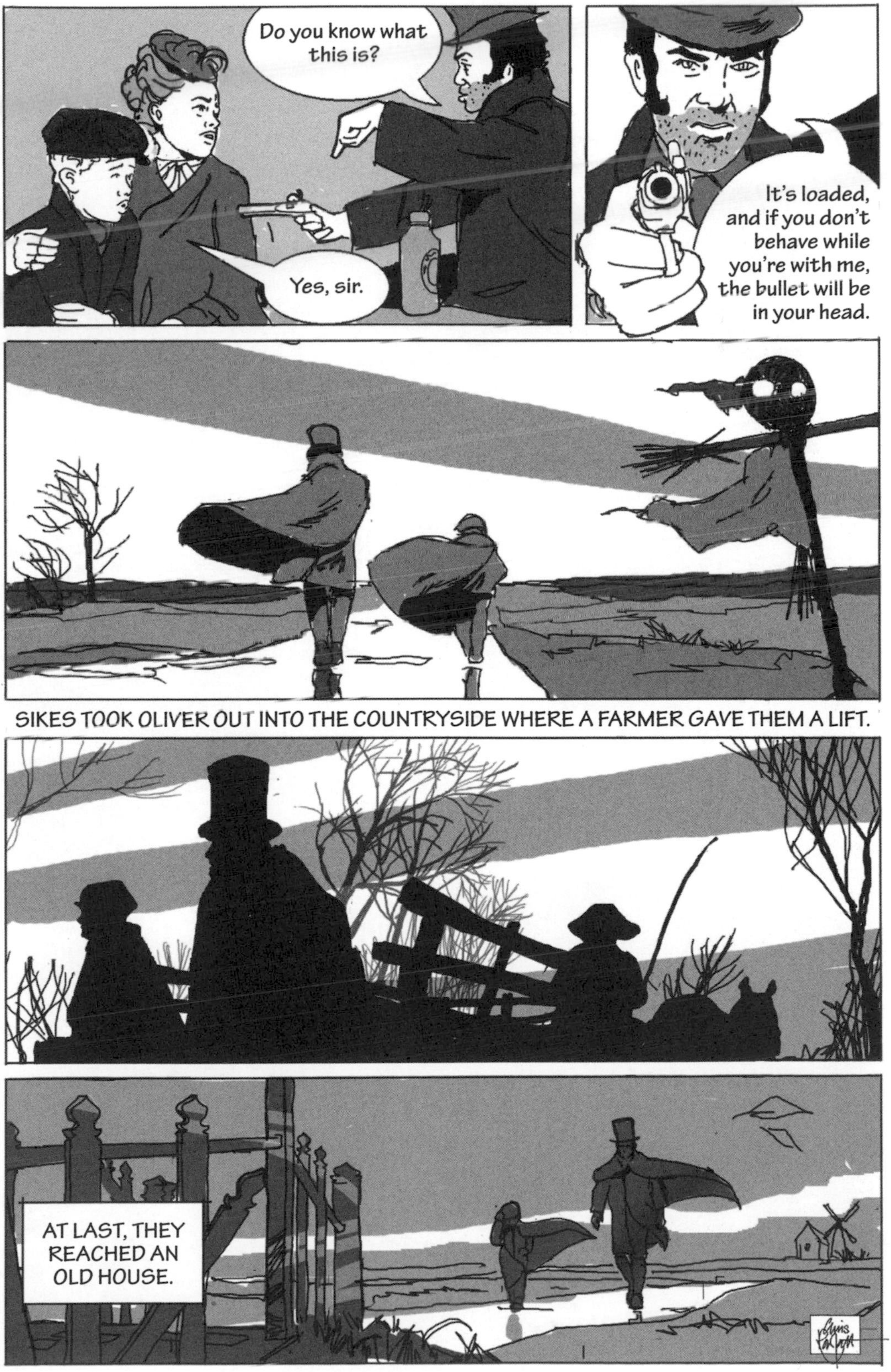
Do you know what this is?
Yes, sir.
It's loaded, and if you don't behave while you're with me, the bullet will be in your head.
SIKES TOOK OLIVER OUT INTO THE COUNTRYSIDE WHERE A FARMER GAVE THEM A LIFT.
AT LAST, THEY REACHED AN OLD HOUSE.

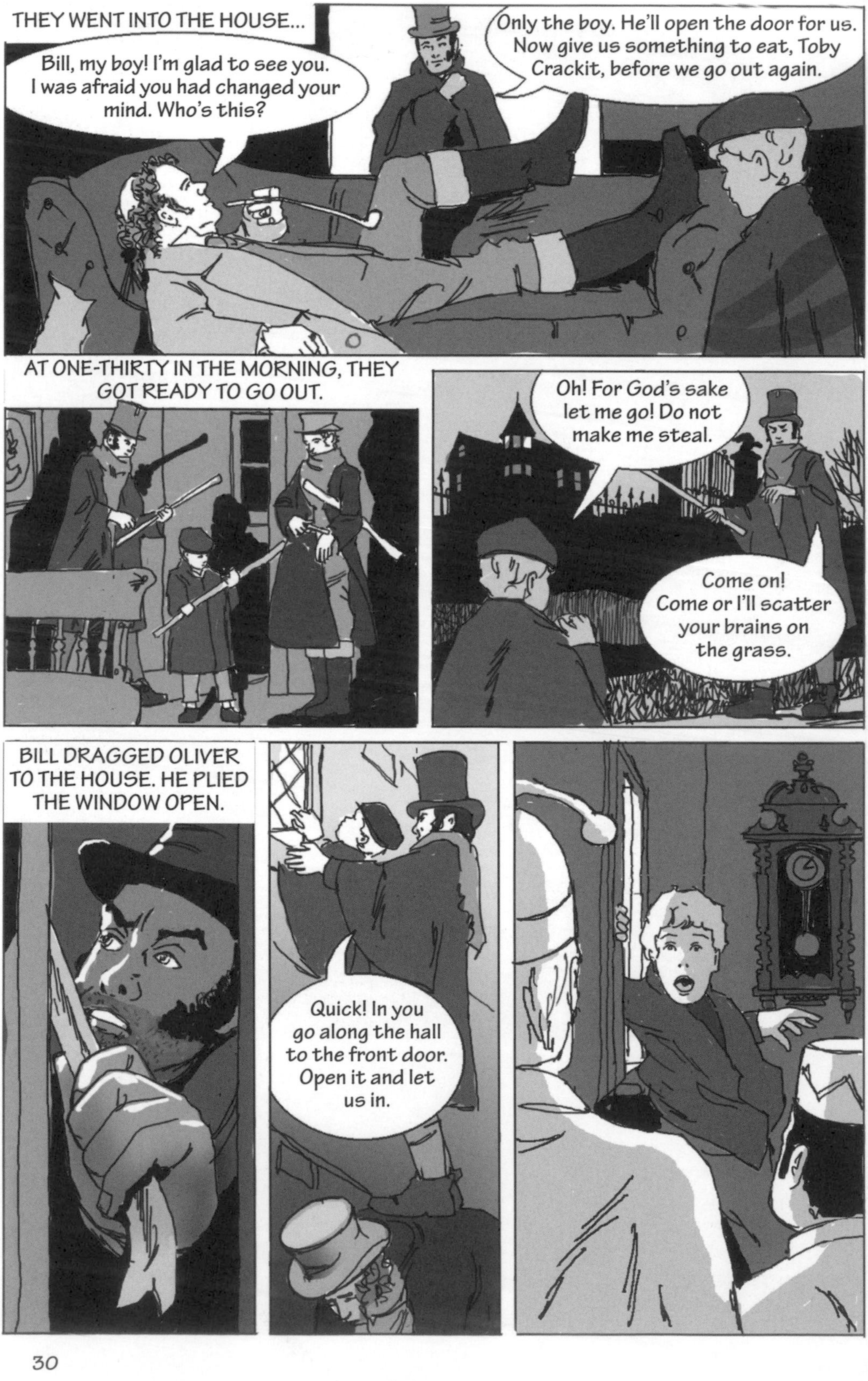
THEY WENT INTO THE HOUSE...
Bill, my boy! I'm glad to see you. I was afraid you had changed your mind. Who's this?
Only the boy. He'll open the door for us. Now give us something to eat, Toby Crackit, before we go out again.
AT ONE-THIRTY IN THE MORNING, THEY GOT READY TO GO OUT.
Oh! For God's sake let me go! Do not make me steal.
Come on! Come or I'll scatter your brains on the grass.
BILL DRAGGED OLIVER TO THE HOUSE. HE PLIED THE WINDOW OPEN.
Quick! In you go along the hall to the front door. Open it and let us in.

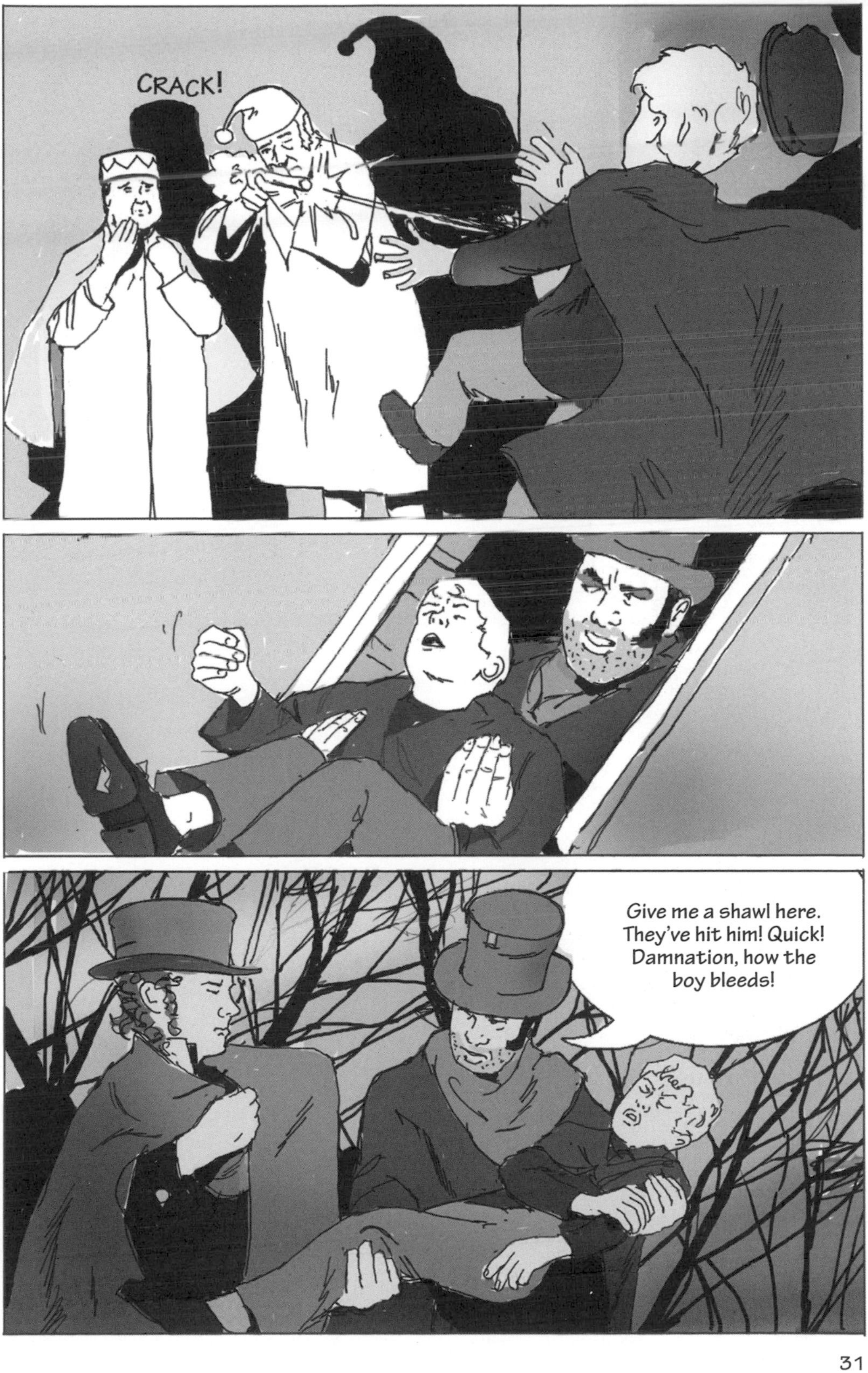
CRACK!
Give me a shawl here. They've hit him! Quick! Damnation, how the boy bleeds!

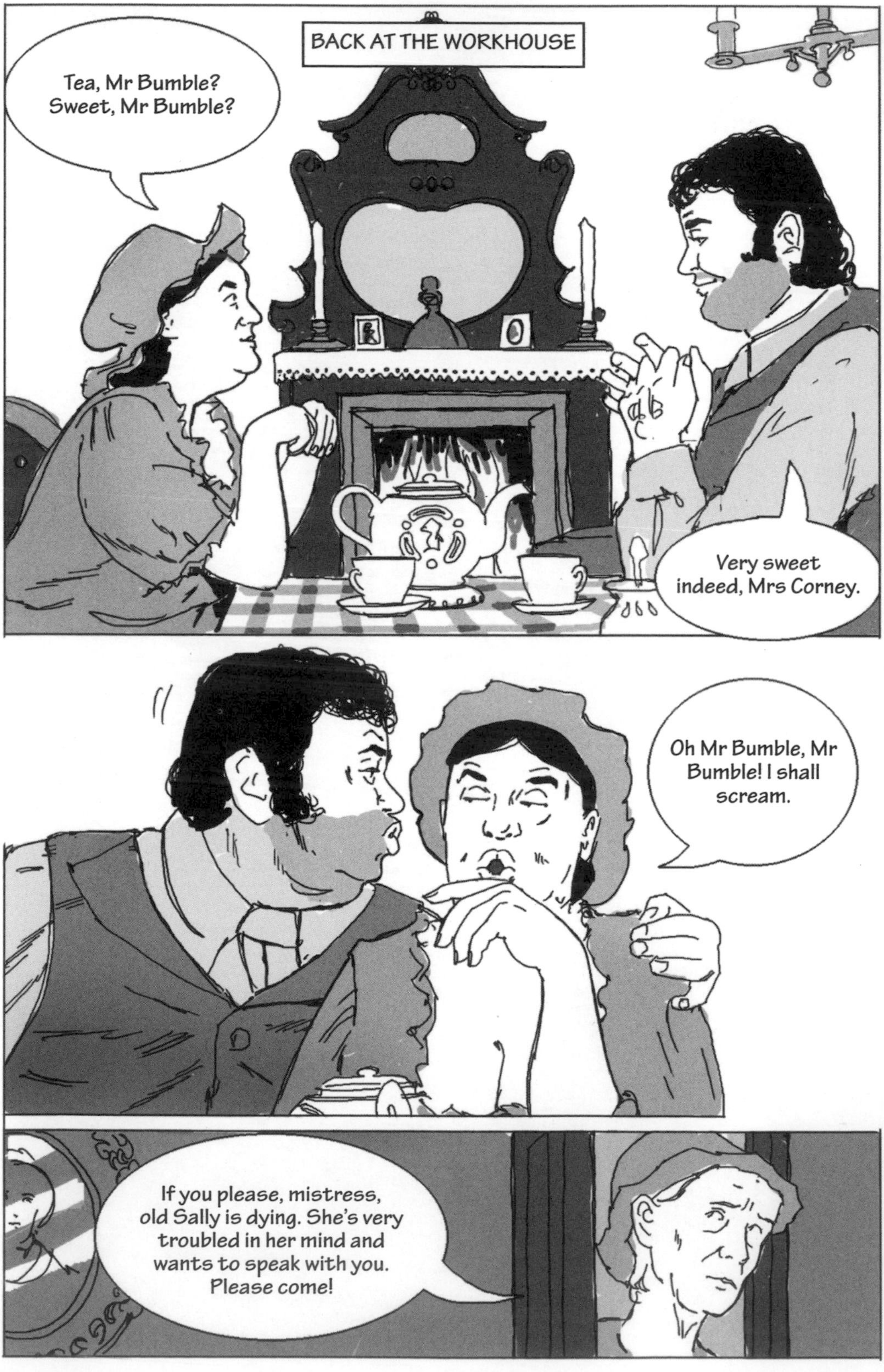
BACK AT THE WORKHOUSE
Tea, Mr Bumble? Sweet, Mr Bumble?
Very sweet indeed, Mrs Corney.
Oh Mr Bumble, Mr Bumble! I shall scream.
If you please, mistress, old Sally is dying. She's very troubled in her mind and wants to speak with you. Please come!

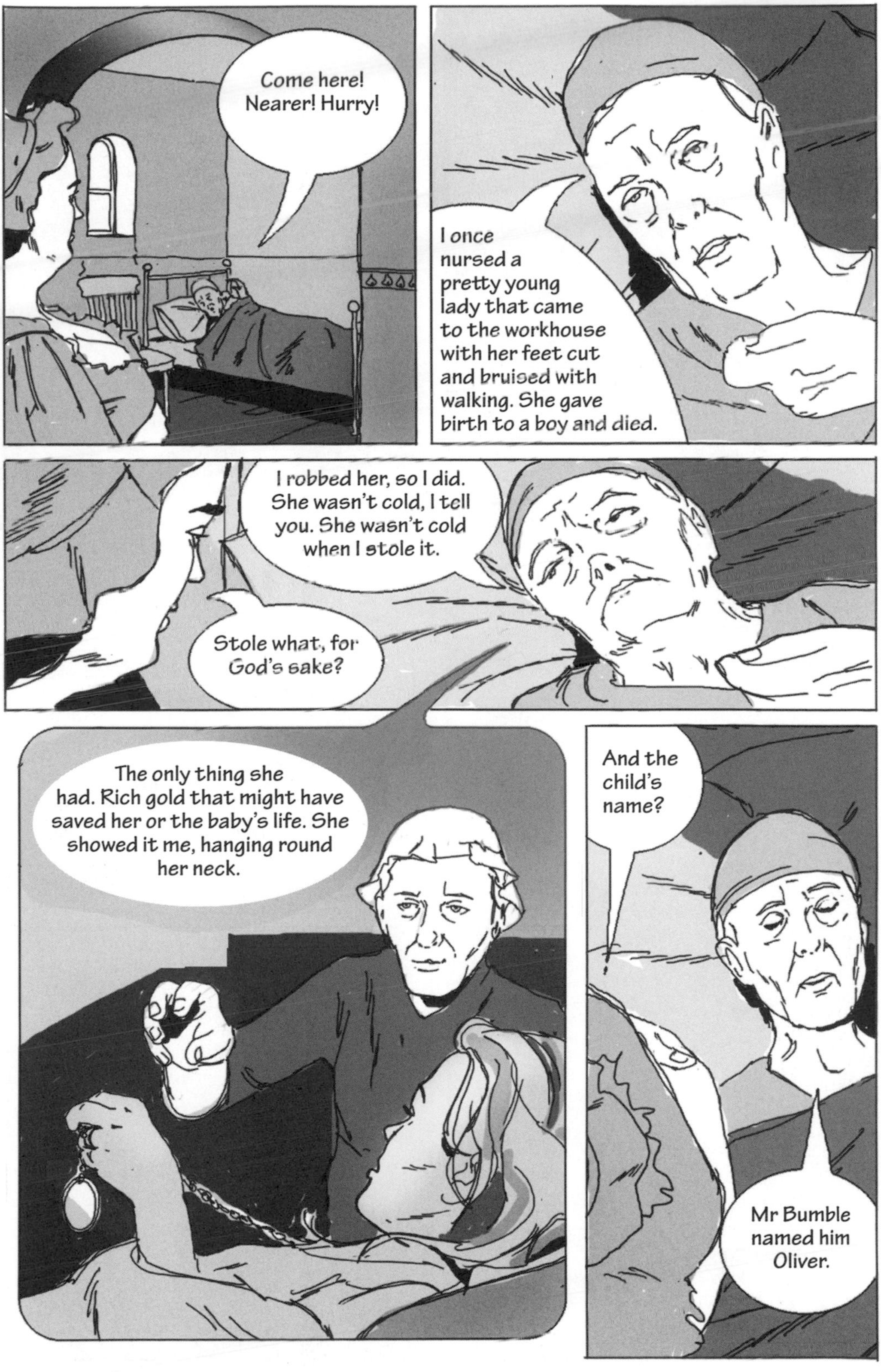

Come here! Nearer! Hurry!
I once nursed a pretty young lady that came to the workhouse with her feet cut and bruised with walking. She gave birth to a boy and died.
I robbed her, so I did. She wasn't cold, I tell you. She wasn't cold when I stole it.
Stole what, for God's sake?
The only thing she had. Rich gold that might have saved her or the baby's life. She showed it me, hanging round her neck.
And the child's name?
Mr Bumble named him Oliver.

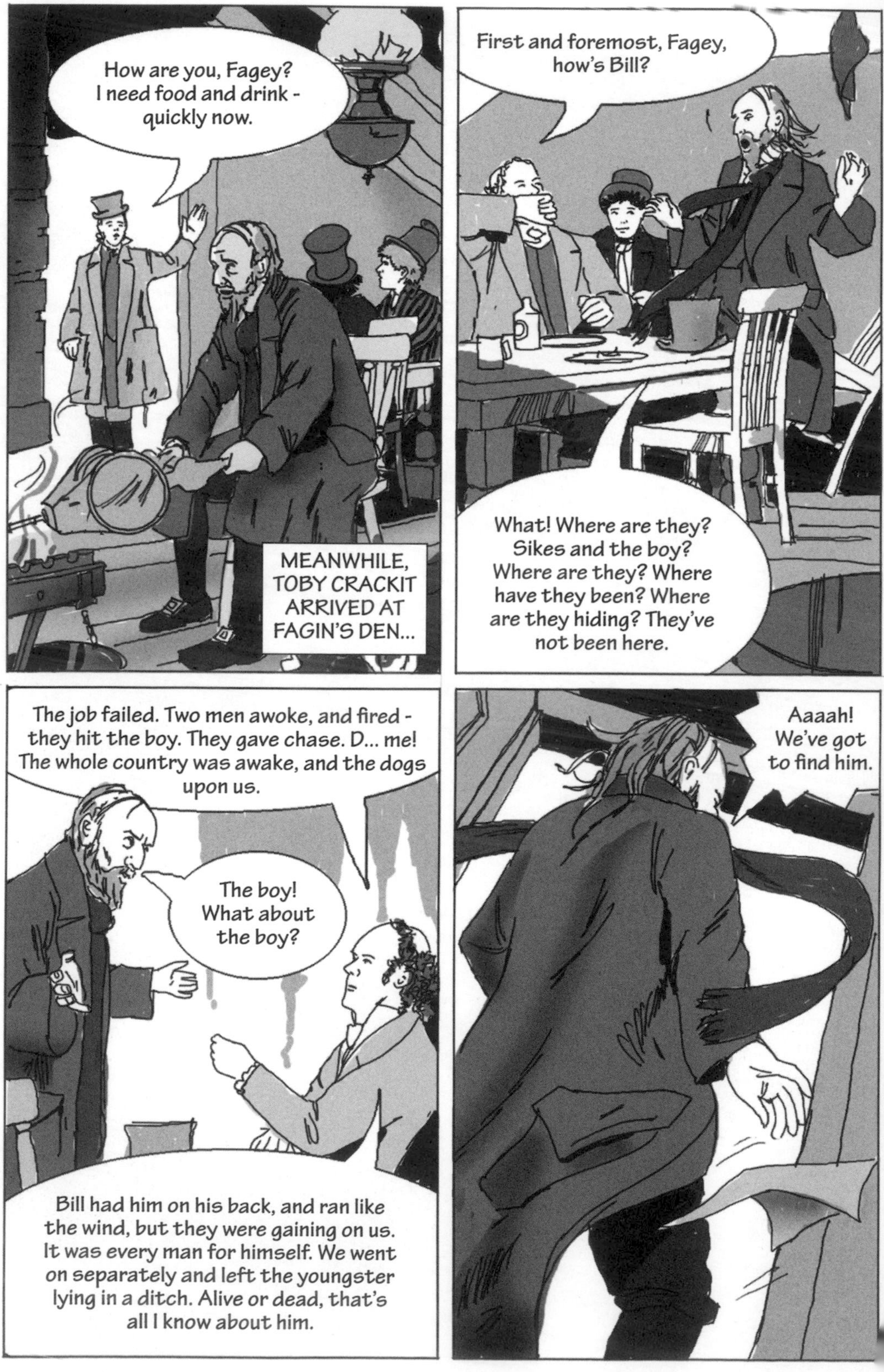
How are you, Fagey? I need food and drink - quickly now.
MEANWHILE, TOBY CRACKIT ARRIVED AT FAGIN'S DEN...
First and foremost, Fagey, how's Bill?
What! Where are they? Sikes and the boy? Where are they? Where have they been? Where are they hiding? They've not been here.
The job failed. Two men awoke, and fired - they hit the boy. They gave chase. D... me! The whole country was awake, and the dogs upon us.
The boy! What about the boy?
Bill had him on his back, and ran like the wind, but they were gaining on us. It was every man for himself. We went on separately and left the youngster lying in a ditch. Alive or dead, that's all I know about him.
Aaaah! We've got to find him.

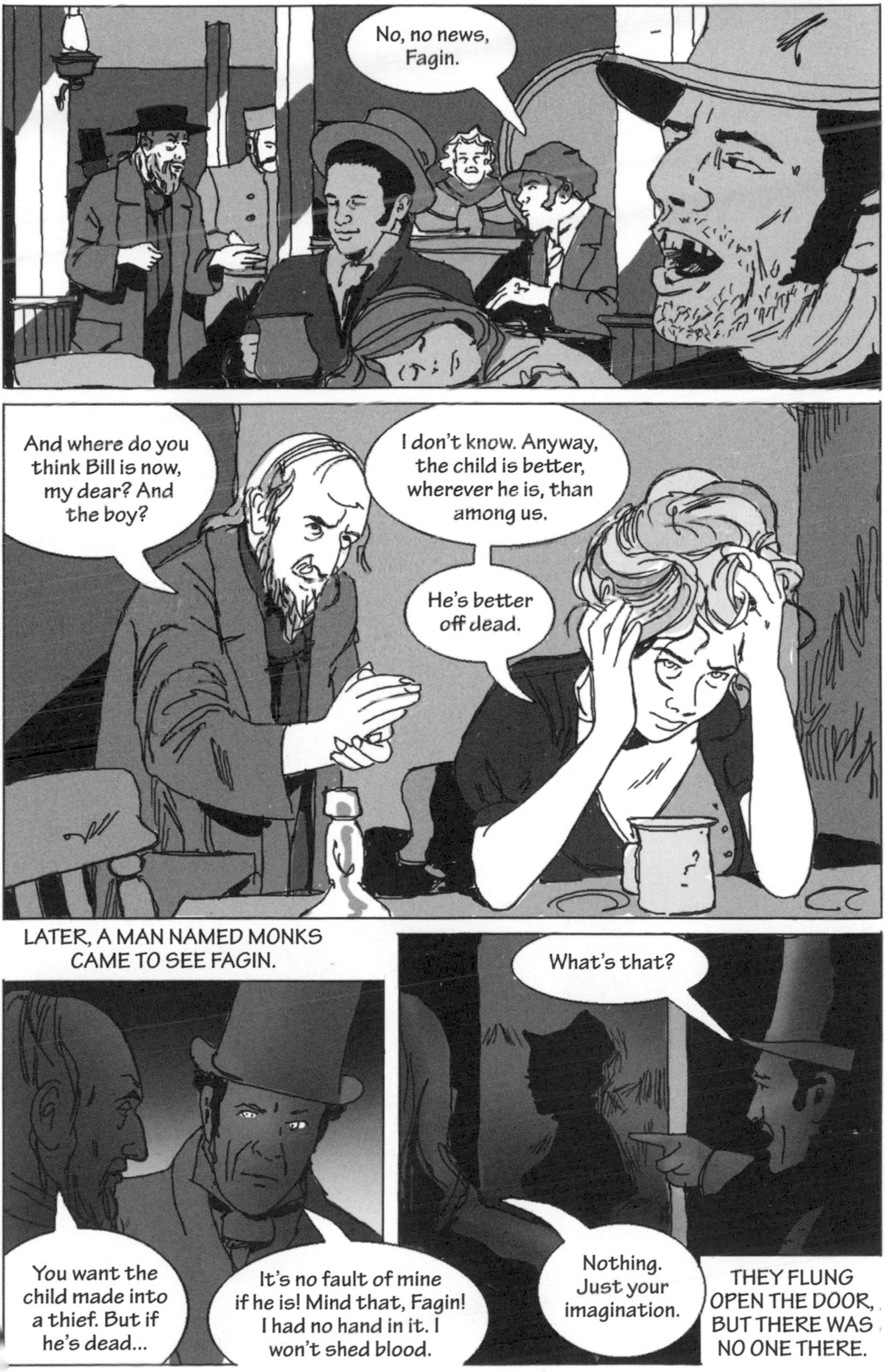

No, no news, Fagin.
And where do you think Bill is now, my dear? And the boy?
I don't know. Anyway, the child is better, wherever he is, than among us.
He's better off dead.
LATER, A MAN NAMED MONKS CAME TO SEE FAGIN.
You want the child made into a thief. But if he's dead...
It's no fault of mine if he is! Mind that, Fagin! I had no hand in it. I won't shed blood.
What's that?
Nothing. Just your imagination.
THEY FLUNG OPEN THE DOOR, BUT THERE WAS NO ONE THERE.

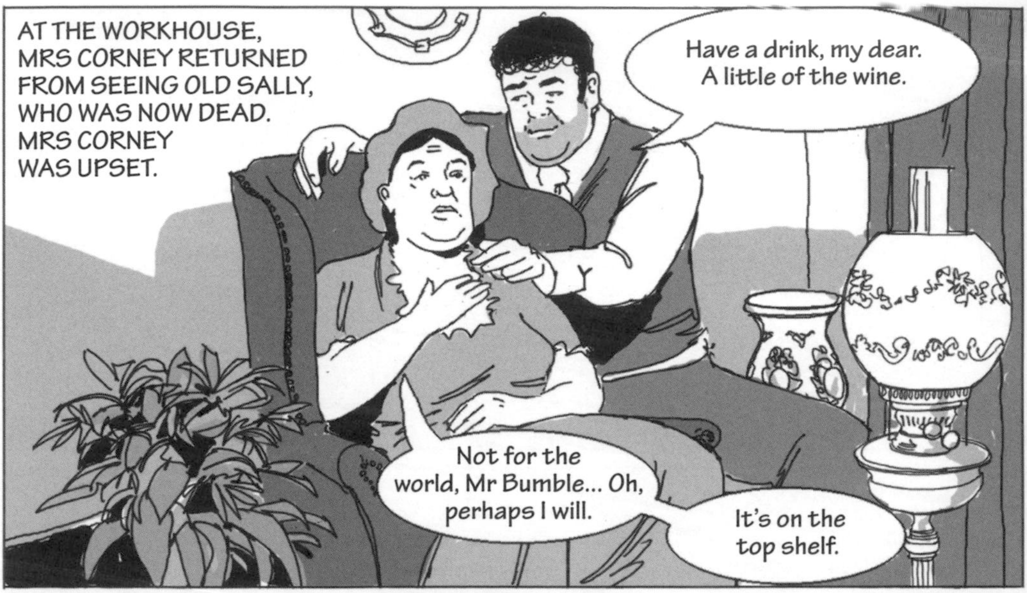
AT THE WORKHOUSE, MRS CORNEY RETURNED FROM SEEING OLD SALLY, WHO WAS NOW DEAD. MRS CORNEY WAS UPSET.
Have a drink, my dear. A little of the wine.
Not for the world, Mr Bumble... Oh, perhaps I will.
It's on the top shelf.

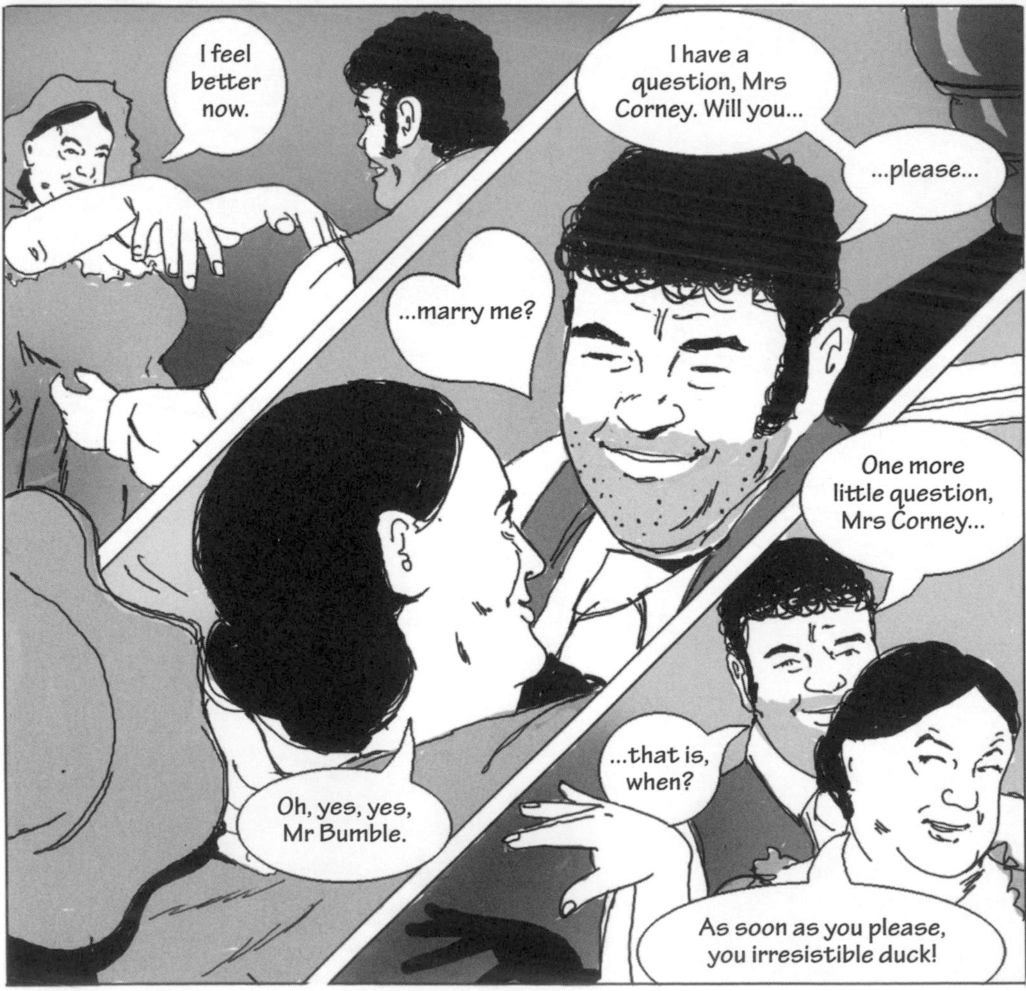
I feel better now.
I have a question, Mrs Corney. Will you...
...please...
...marry me?
Oh, yes, yes, Mr Bumble.
One more little question, Mrs Corney...
...that is, when?
As soon as you please, you irresistible duck!

AFTER THE FAILED BURGLARY, BILL SIKES AND TOBY CRACKIT RAN FOR THEIR LIVES. SIKES CARRIED THE WOUNDED OLIVER...

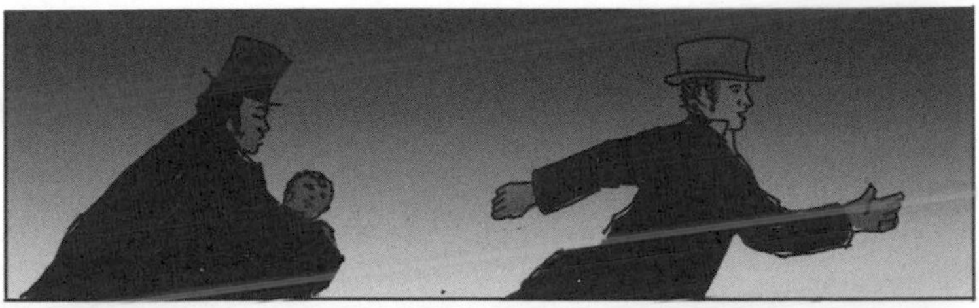

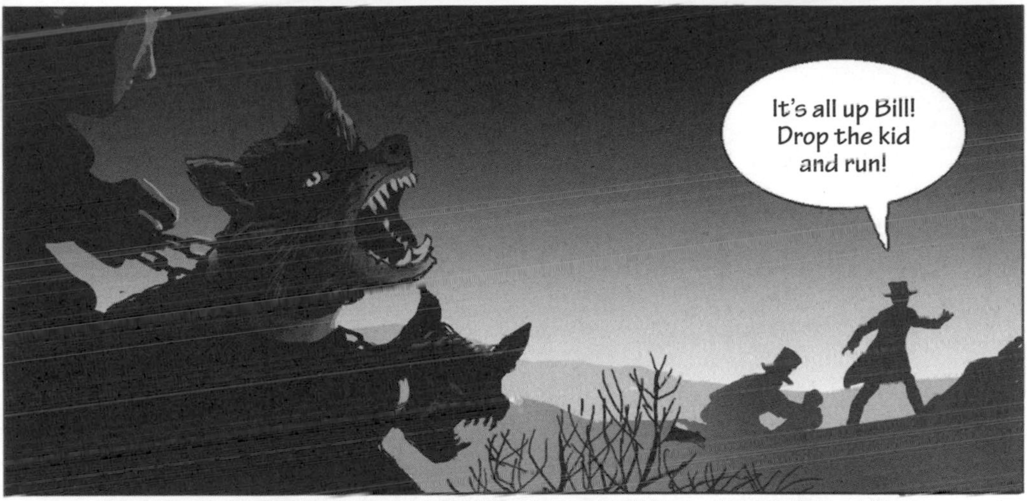
It's all up Bill! Drop the kid and run!

THEY RAN, LEAVING OLIVER BEHIND, UNCONSCIOUS. AT LAST HE AWOKE. THE PURSUERS HAD GONE AWAY.

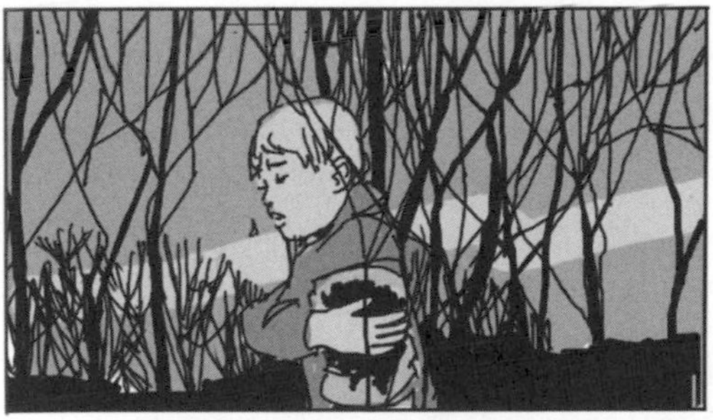

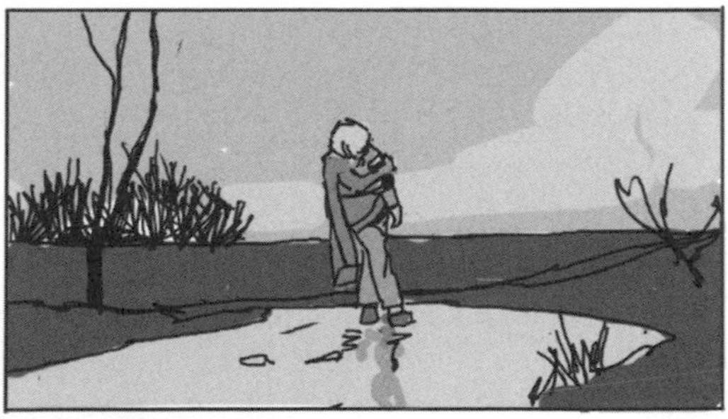

HE CAME TO A BIG HOUSE, AND GAVE A FAINT KNOCK AT THE DOOR.

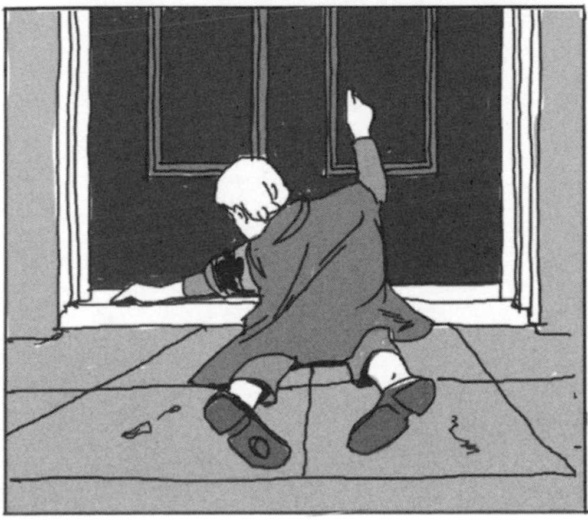

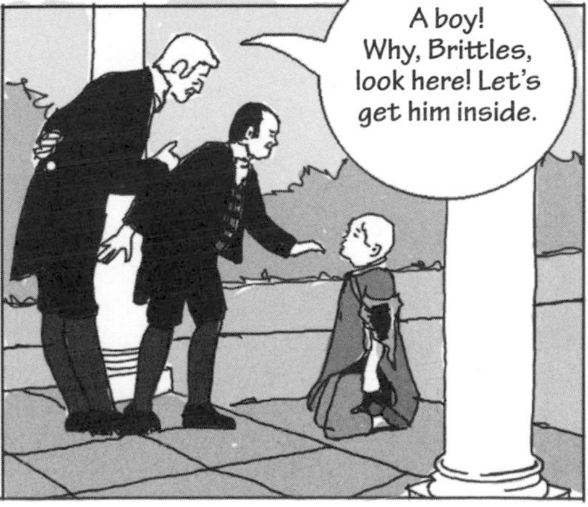
A boy! Why, Brittles, look here! Let's get him inside.

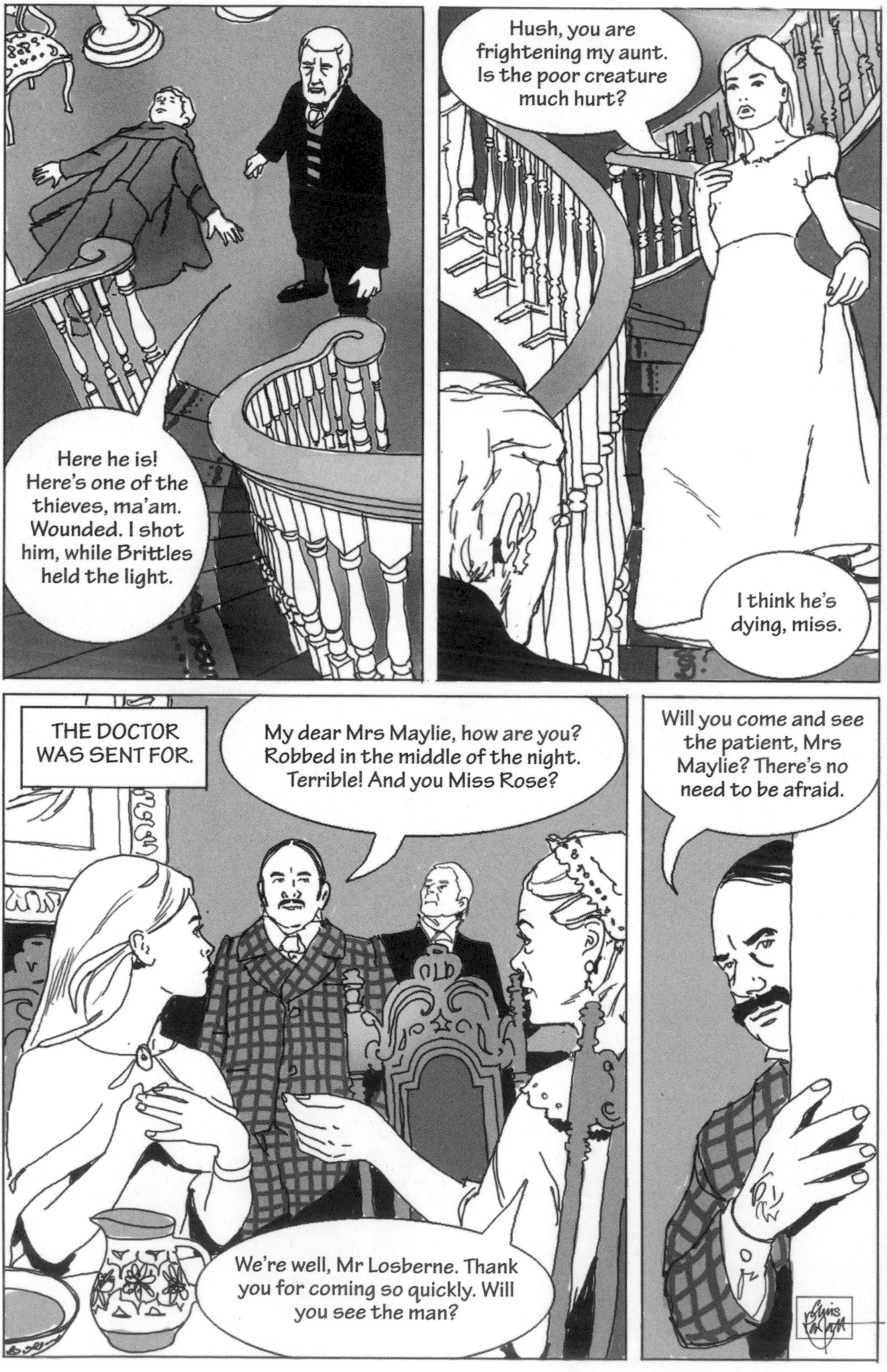
Here he is! Here's one of the thieves, ma'am. Wounded. I shot him, while Brittles held the light.
Hush, you are frightening my aunt. Is the poor creature much hurt?
I think he's dying, miss.
THE DOCTOR WAS SENT FOR.
My dear Mrs Maylie, how are you? Robbed in the middle of the night. Terrible! And you Miss Rose?
We're well, Mr Losberne. Thank you for coming so quickly. Will you see the man?
Will you come and see the patient, Mrs Maylie? There's no need to be afraid.

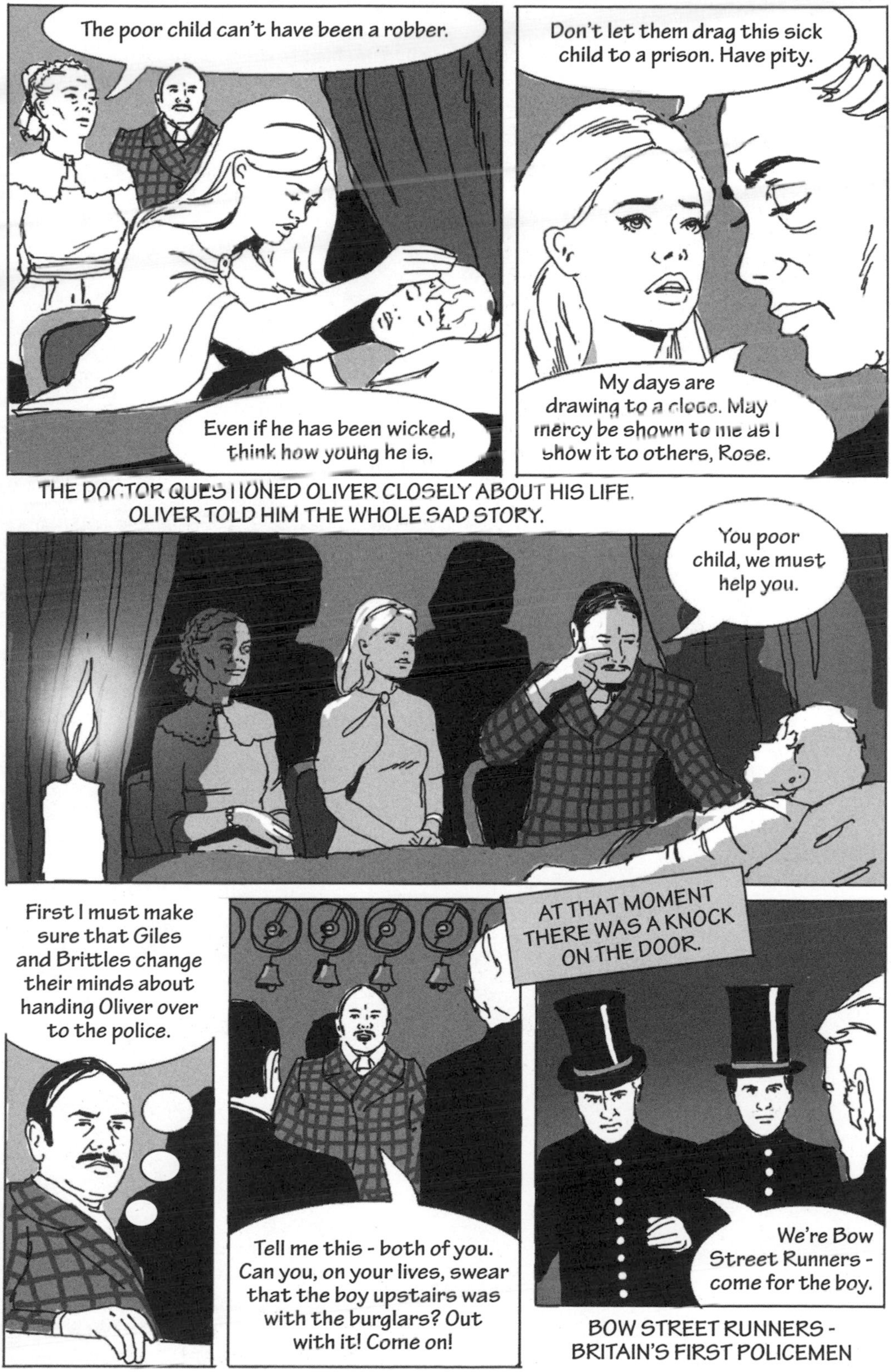
The poor child can't have been a robber.
Even if he has been wicked, think how young he is.
Don't let them drag this sick child to a prison. Have pity.
My days are drawing to a close. May mercy be shown to me as I show it to others, Rose.
THE DOCTOR QUESTIONED OLIVER CLOSELY ABOUT HIS LIFE. OLIVER TOLD HIM THE WHOLE SAD STORY.
You poor child, we must help you.
First I must make sure that Giles and Brittles change their minds about handing Oliver over to the police.
Tell me this - both of you. Can you, on your lives, swear that the boy upstairs was with the burglars? Out with it! Come on!
AT THAT MOMENT THERE WAS A KNOCK ON THE DOOR.
We're Bow Street Runners - come for the boy.
BOW STREET RUNNERS - BRITAIN'S FIRST POLICEMEN

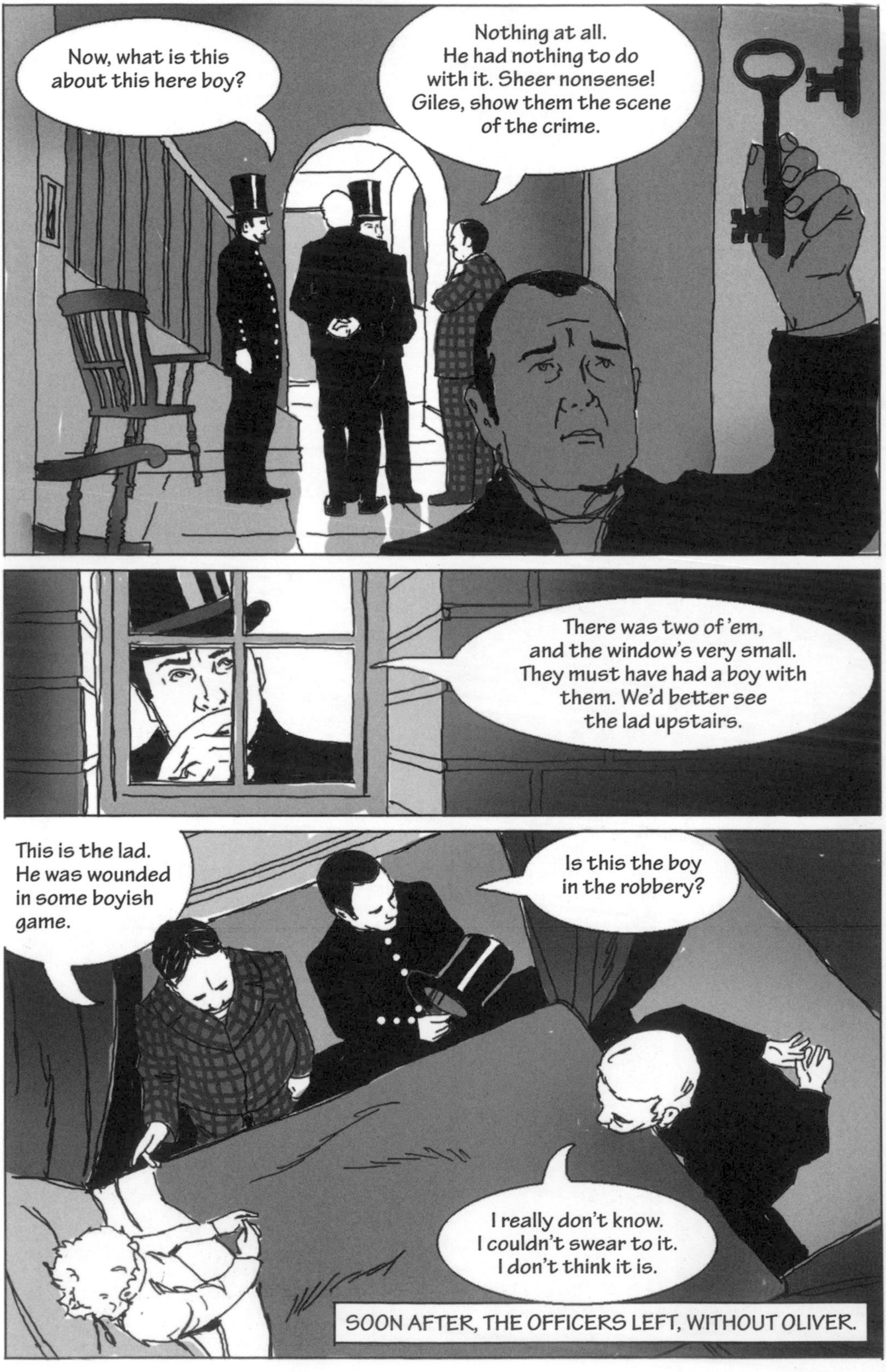
Now, what is this about this here boy?
Nothing at all. He had nothing to do with it. Sheer nonsense! Giles, show them the scene of the crime.
There was two of 'em, and the window's very small. They must have had a boy with them. We'd better see the lad upstairs.
This is the lad. He was wounded in some boyish game.
Is this the boy in the robbery?
I really don't know. I couldn't swear to it. I don't think it is.
SOON AFTER, THE OFFICERS LEFT, WITHOUT OLIVER.

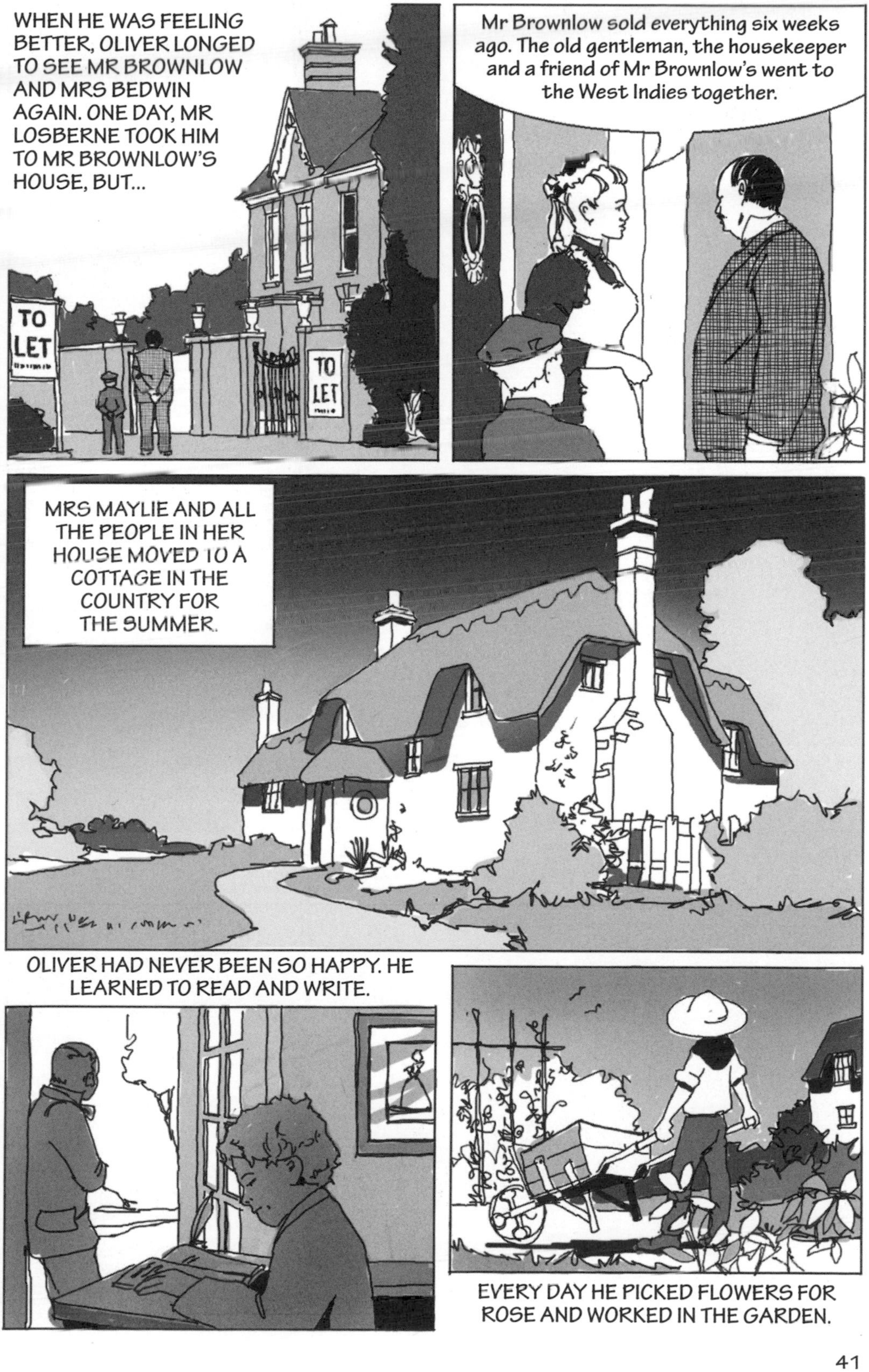
WHEN HE WAS FEELING BETTER, OLIVER LONGED TO SEE MR BROWNLOW AND MRS BEDWIN AGAIN. ONE DAY, MR LOSBERNE TOOK HIM TO MR BROWNLOW'S HOUSE, BUT...
TO LET
TO LET
Mr Brownlow sold everything six weeks ago. The old gentleman, the housekeeper and a friend of Mr Brownlow's went to the West Indies together.
MRS MAYLIE AND ALL THE PEOPLE IN HER HOUSE MOVED TO A COTTAGE IN THE COUNTRY FOR THE SUMMER.
OLIVER HAD NEVER BEEN SO HAPPY. HE LEARNED TO READ AND WRITE.
EVERY DAY HE PICKED FLOWERS FOR ROSE AND WORKED IN THE GARDEN.

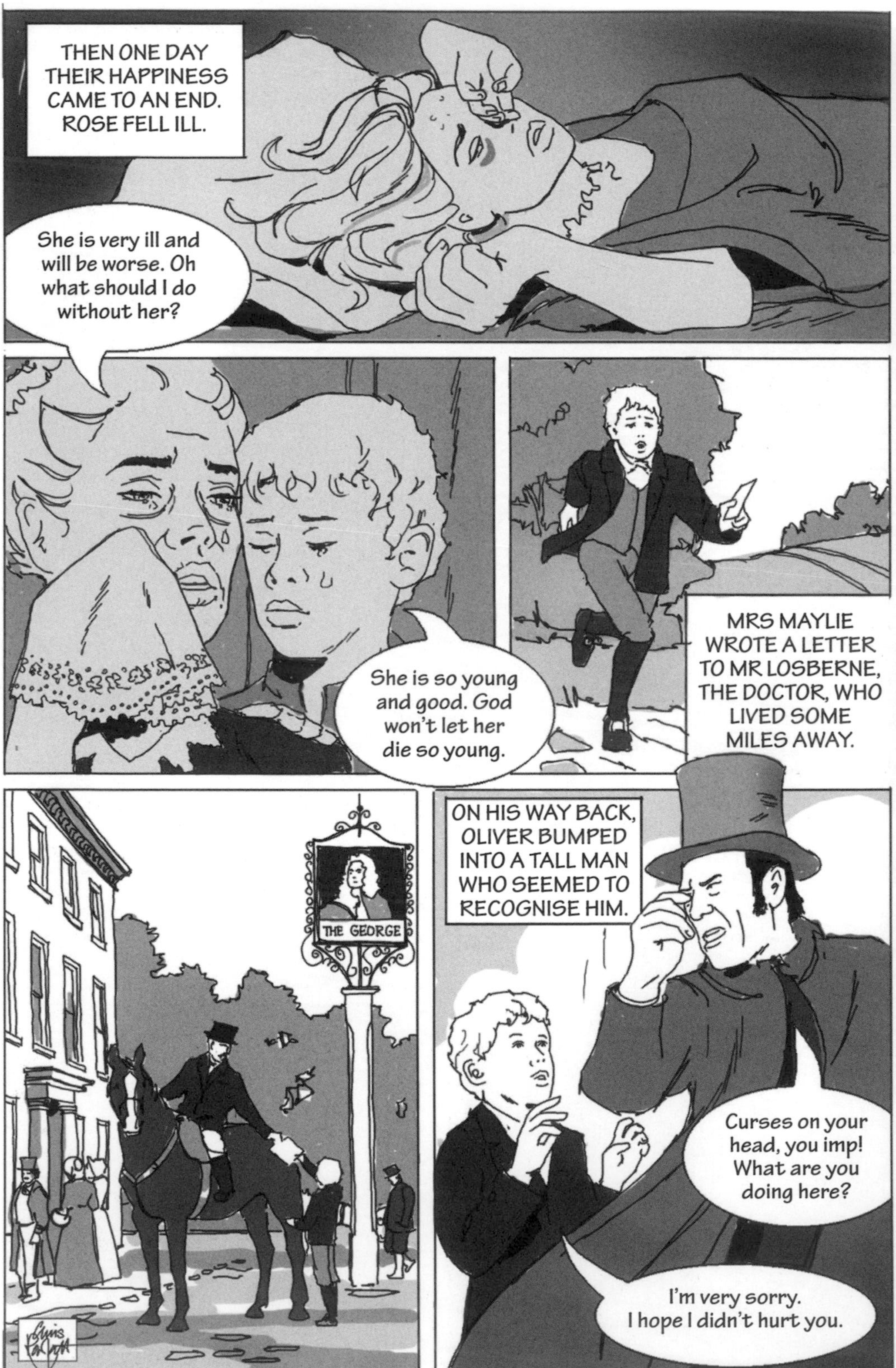
THEN ONE DAY THEIR HAPPINESS CAME TO AN END. ROSE FELL ILL.
She is very ill and will be worse. Oh what should I do without her?
She is so young and good. God won't let her die so young.
MRS MAYLIE WROTE A LETTER TO MR LOSBERNE, THE DOCTOR, WHO LIVED SOME MILES AWAY.
THE GEORGE
ON HIS WAY BACK, OLIVER BUMPED INTO A TALL MAN WHO SEEMED TO RECOGNISE HIM.
Curses on your head, you imp! What are you doing here?
I'm very sorry. I hope I didn't hurt you.

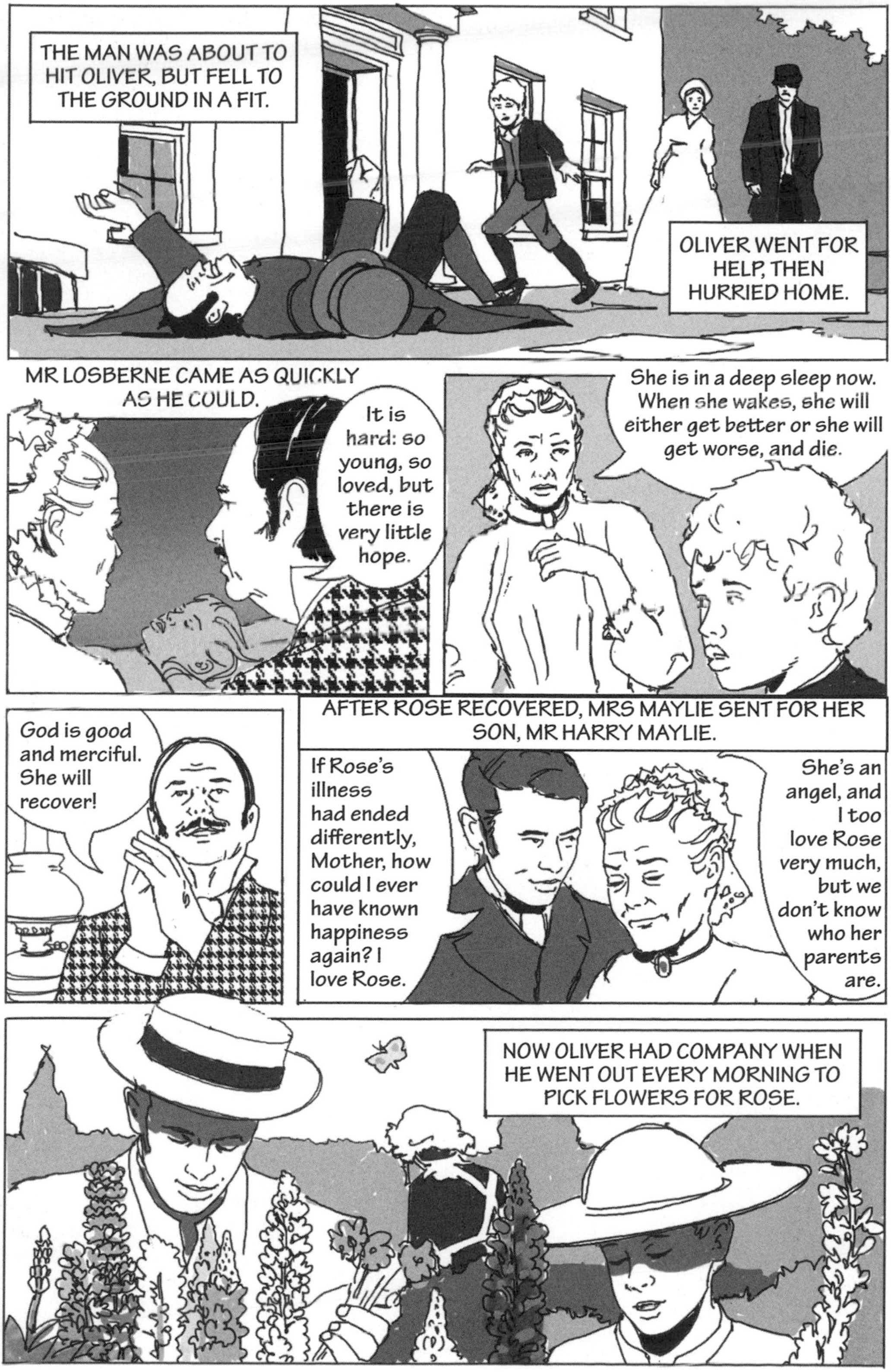
THE MAN WAS ABOUT TO HIT OLIVER, BUT FELL TO THE GROUND IN A FIT.
OLIVER WENT FOR HELP, THEN HURRIED HOME.
MR LOSBERNE CAME AS QUICKLY AS HE COULD.
It is hard: so young, so loved, but there is very little hope.
She is in a deep sleep now. When she wakes, she will either get better or she will get worse, and die.
God is good and merciful. She will recover!
AFTER ROSE RECOVERED, MRS MAYLIE SENT FOR HER SON, MR HARRY MAYLIE.
If Rose's illness had ended differently, Mother, how could I ever have known happiness again? I love Rose.
She's an angel, and I too love Rose very much, but we don't know who her parents are.
NOW OLIVER HAD COMPANY WHEN HE WENT OUT EVERY MORNING TO PICK FLOWERS FOR ROSE.

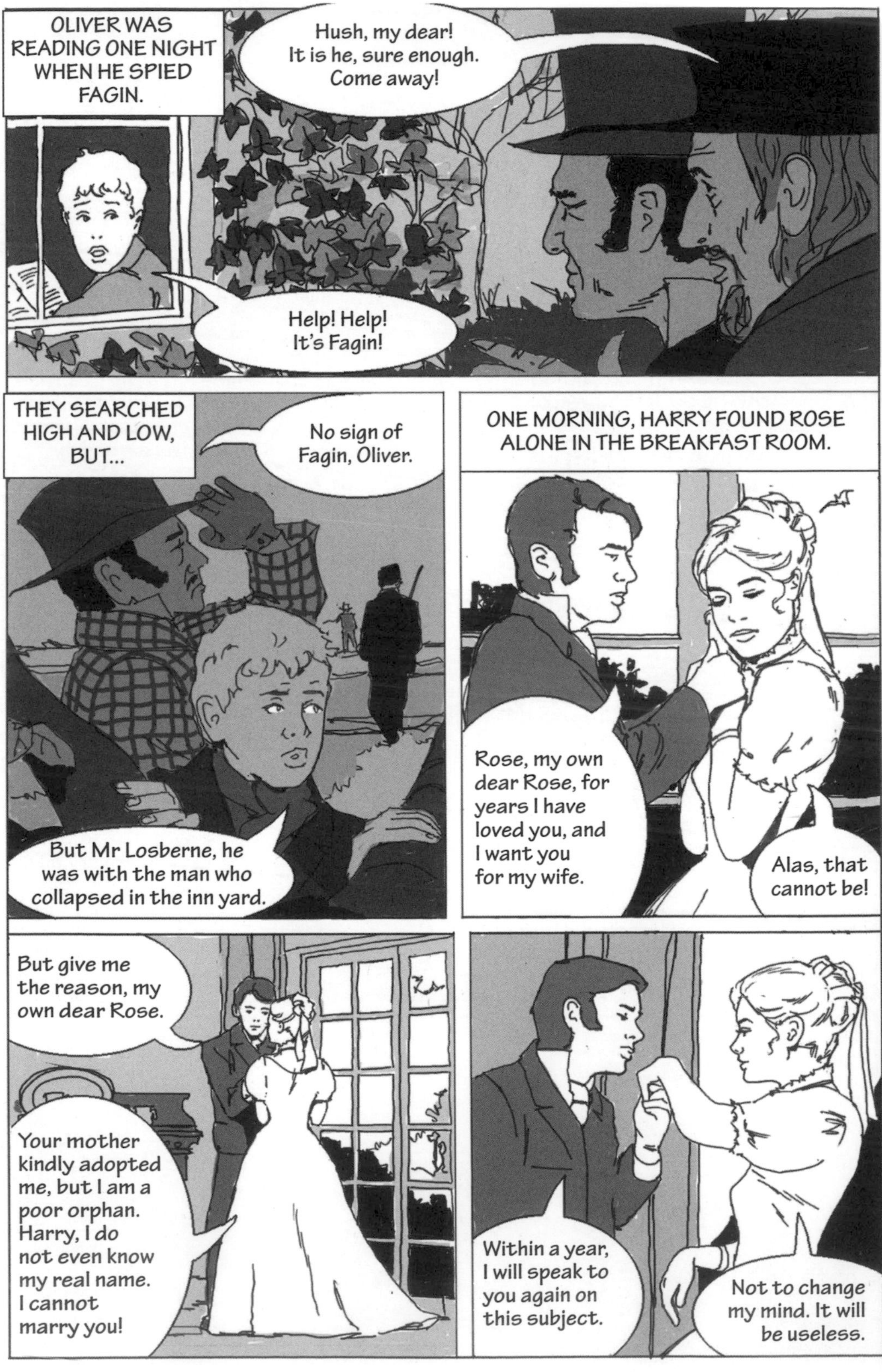
OLIVER WAS READING ONE NIGHT WHEN HE SPIED FAGIN.
Hush, my dear! It is he, sure enough. Come away!
Help! Help! It's Fagin!
THEY SEARCHED HIGH AND LOW, BUT...
No sign of Fagin, Oliver.
But Mr Losberne, he was with the man who collapsed in the inn yard.
ONE MORNING, HARRY FOUND ROSE ALONE IN THE BREAKFAST ROOM.
Rose, my own dear Rose, for years I have loved you, and I want you for my wife.
Alas, that cannot be!
But give me the reason, my own dear Rose.
Your mother kindly adopted me, but I am a poor orphan. Harry, I do not even know my real name. I cannot marry you!
Within a year, I will speak to you again on this subject.
Not to change my mind. It will be useless.

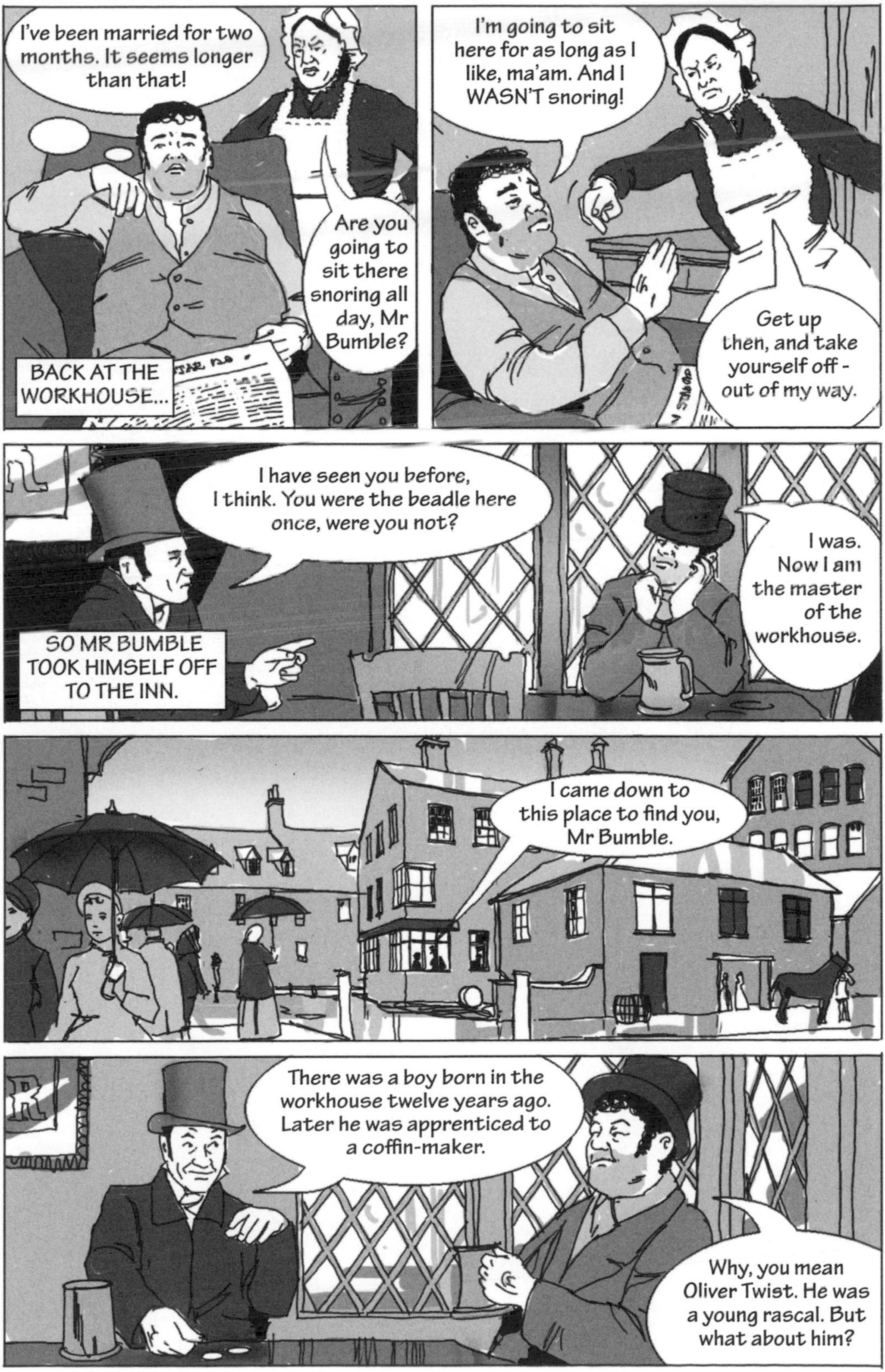
BACK AT THE WORKHOUSE...
I've been married for two months. It seems longer than that!
Are you going to sit there snoring all day, Mr Bumble?
I'm going to sit here for as long as I like, ma'am. And I WASN'T snoring!
Get up then, and take yourself off - out of my way.
SO MR BUMBLE TOOK HIMSELF OFF TO THE INN.
I have seen you before, I think. You were the beadle here once, were you not?
I was. Now I am the master of the workhouse.
I came down to this place to find you, Mr Bumble.
There was a boy born in the workhouse twelve years ago. Later he was apprenticed to a coffin-maker.
Why, you mean Oliver Twist. He was a young rascal. But what about him?

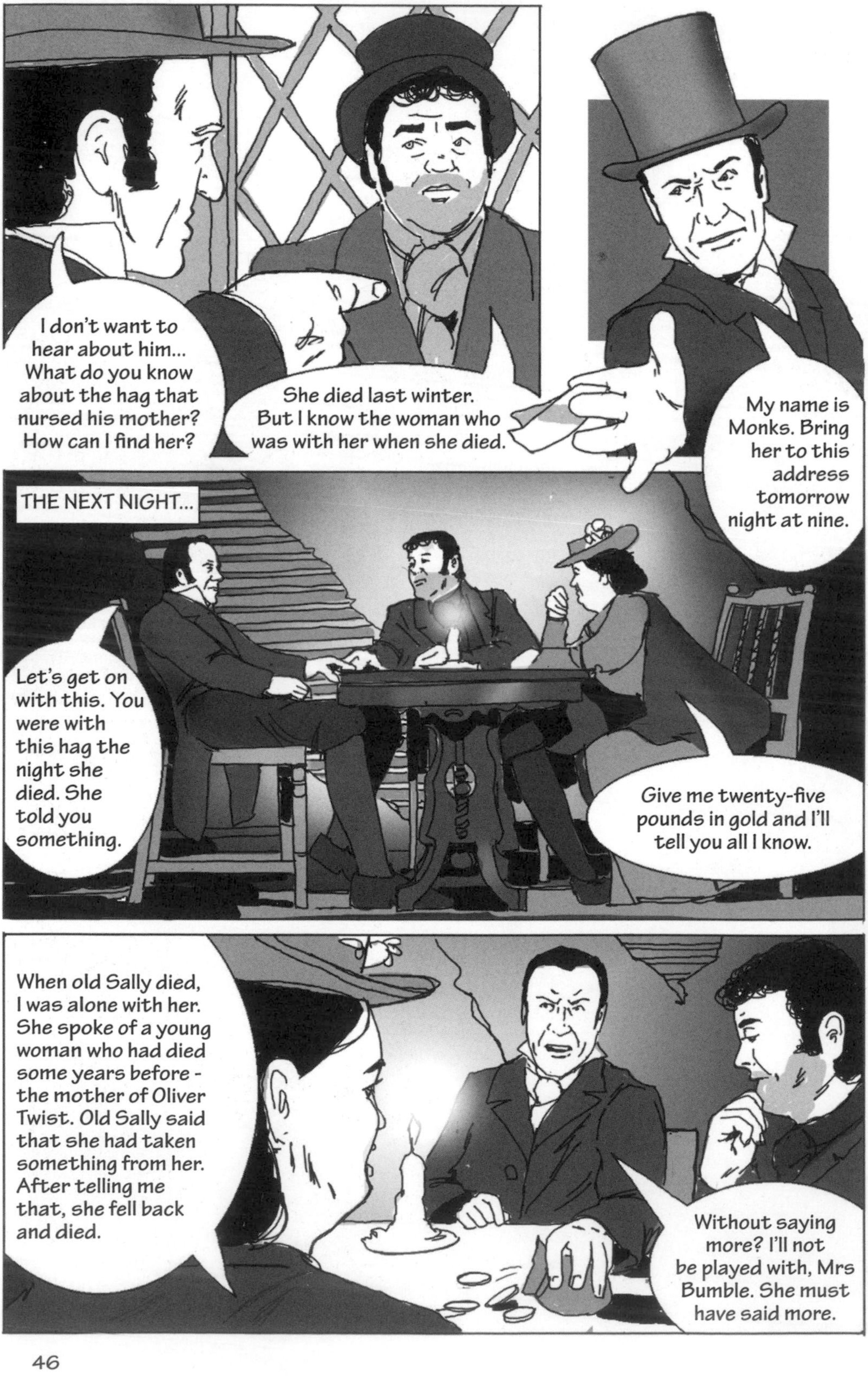

I don't want to hear about him... What do you know about the hag that nursed his mother? How can I find her?
She died last winter. But I know the woman who was with her when she died.
My name is Monks. Bring her to this address tomorrow night at nine.
THE NEXT NIGHT...
Let's get on with this. You were with this hag the night she died. She told you something.
Give me twenty-five pounds in gold and I'll tell you all I know.
When old Sally died, I was alone with her. She spoke of a young woman who had died some years before - the mother of Oliver Twist. Old Sally said that she had taken something from her. After telling me that, she fell back and died.
Without saying more? I'll not be played with, Mrs Bumble. She must have said more.

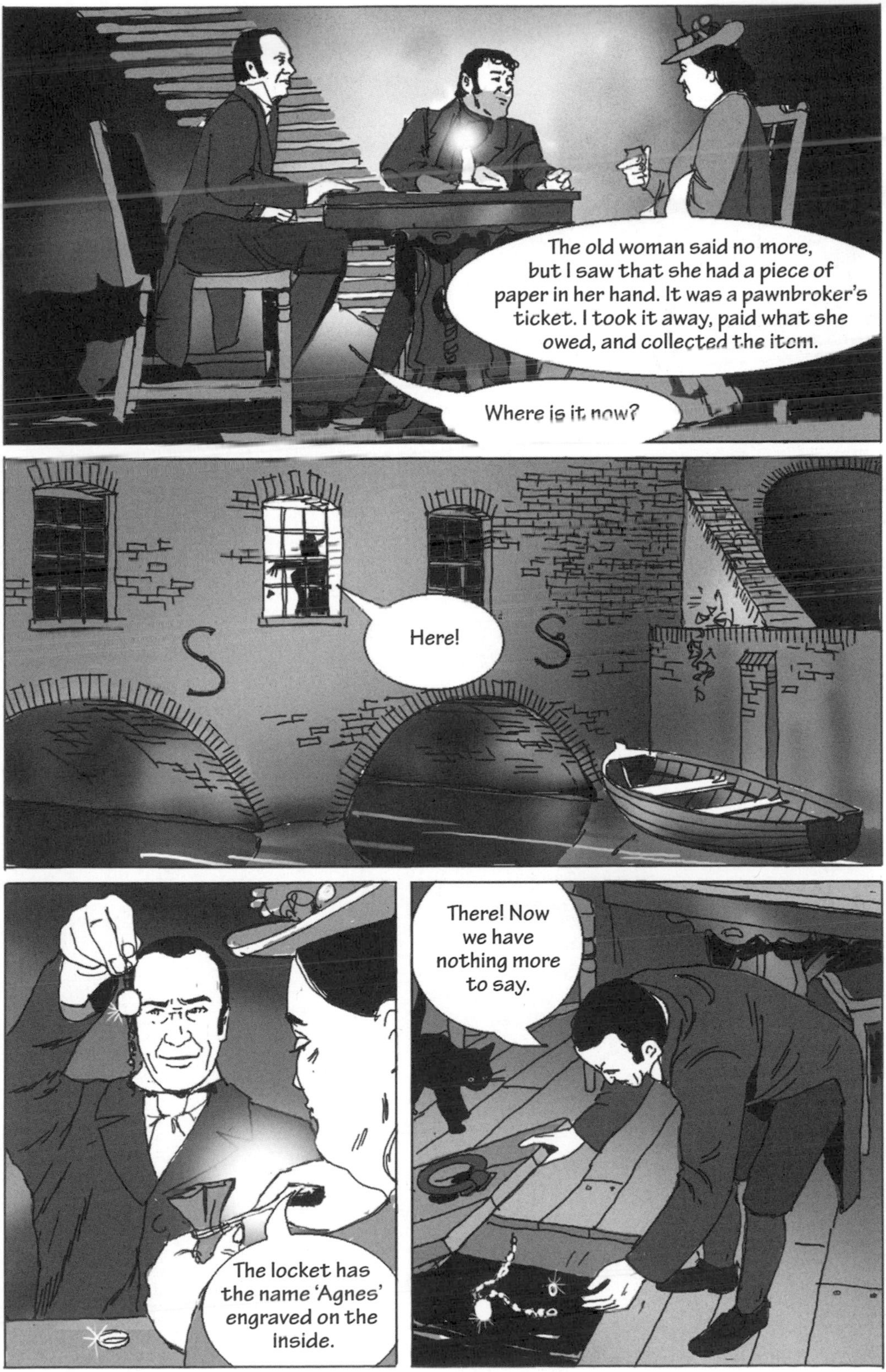
The old woman said no more, but I saw that she had a piece of paper in her hand. It was a pawnbroker's ticket. I took it away, paid what she owed, and collected the item.
Where is it now?
Here!
The locket has the name 'Agnes' engraved on the inside.
There! Now we have nothing more to say.

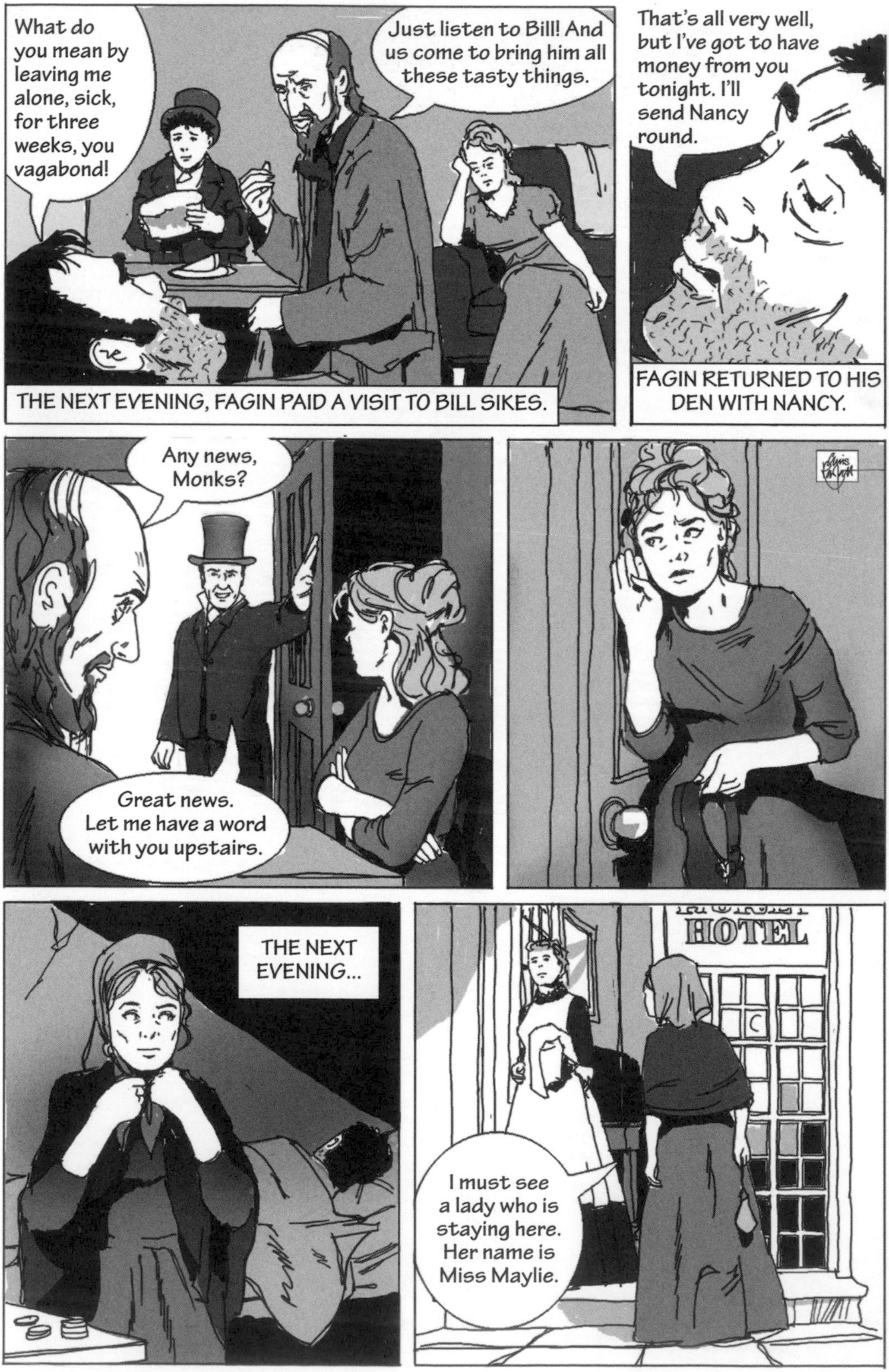
What do you mean by leaving me alone, sick, for three weeks, you vagabond!
Just listen to Bill! And us come to bring him all these tasty things.
THE NEXT EVENING, FAGIN PAID A VISIT TO BILL SIKES.
That's all very well, but I've got to have money from you tonight. I'll send Nancy round.
FAGIN RETURNED TO HIS DEN WITH NANCY.
Any news, Monks?
Great news. Let me have a word with you upstairs.
THE NEXT EVENING...
HOTEL
I must see a lady who is staying here. Her name is Miss Maylie.

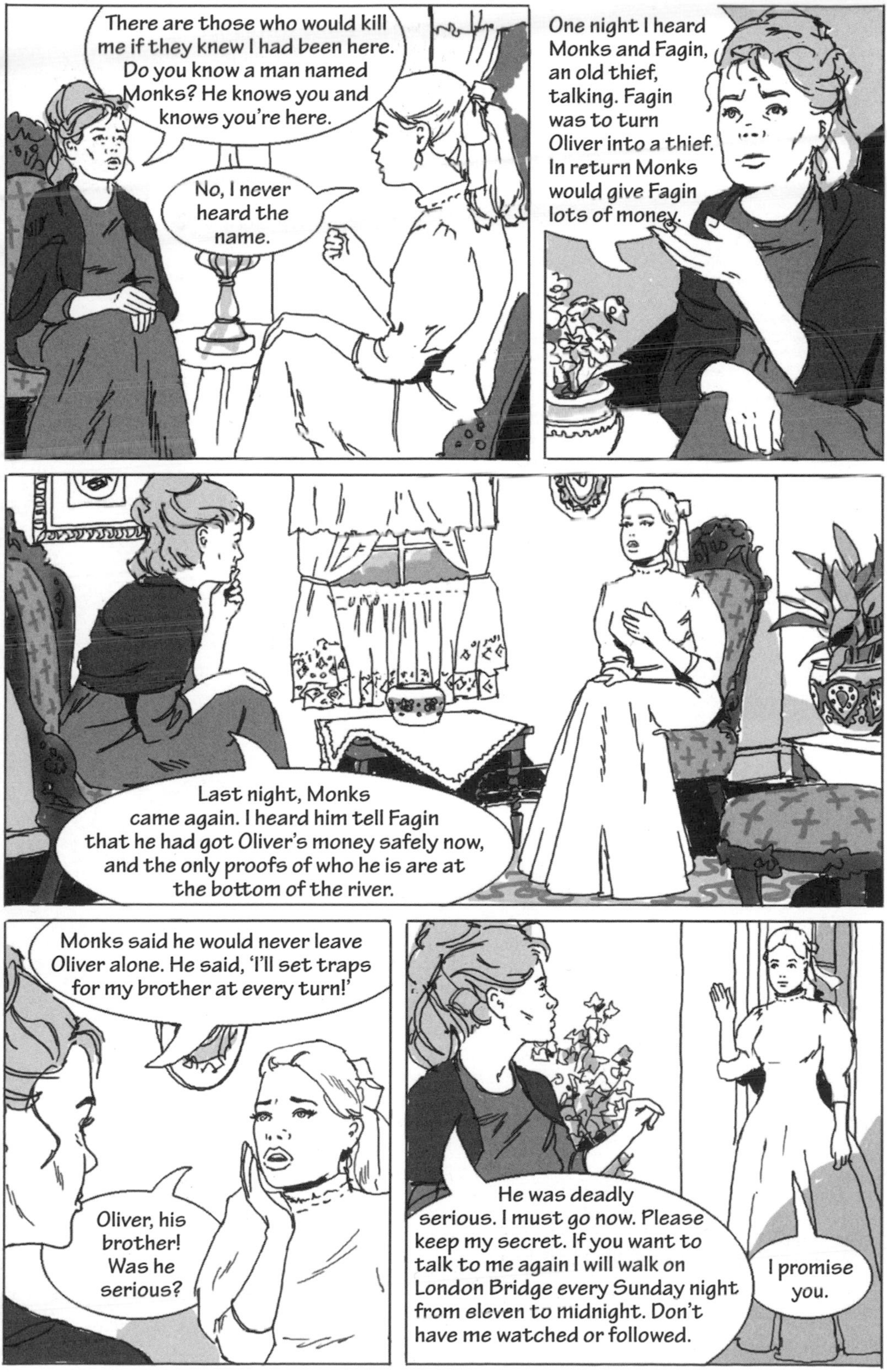
There are those who would kill me if they knew I had been here. Do you know a man named Monks? He knows you and knows you're here.
No, I never heard the name.
One night I heard Monks and Fagin, an old thief, talking. Fagin was to turn Oliver into a thief. In return Monks would give Fagin lots of money.
Last night, Monks came again. I heard him tell Fagin that he had got Oliver's money safely now, and the only proofs of who he is are at the bottom of the river.
Monks said he would never leave Oliver alone. He said, 'I'll set traps for my brother at every turn!'
Oliver, his brother! Was he serious?
He was deadly serious. I must go now. Please keep my secret. If you want to talk to me again I will walk on London Bridge every Sunday night from eleven to midnight. Don't have me watched or followed.
I promise you.

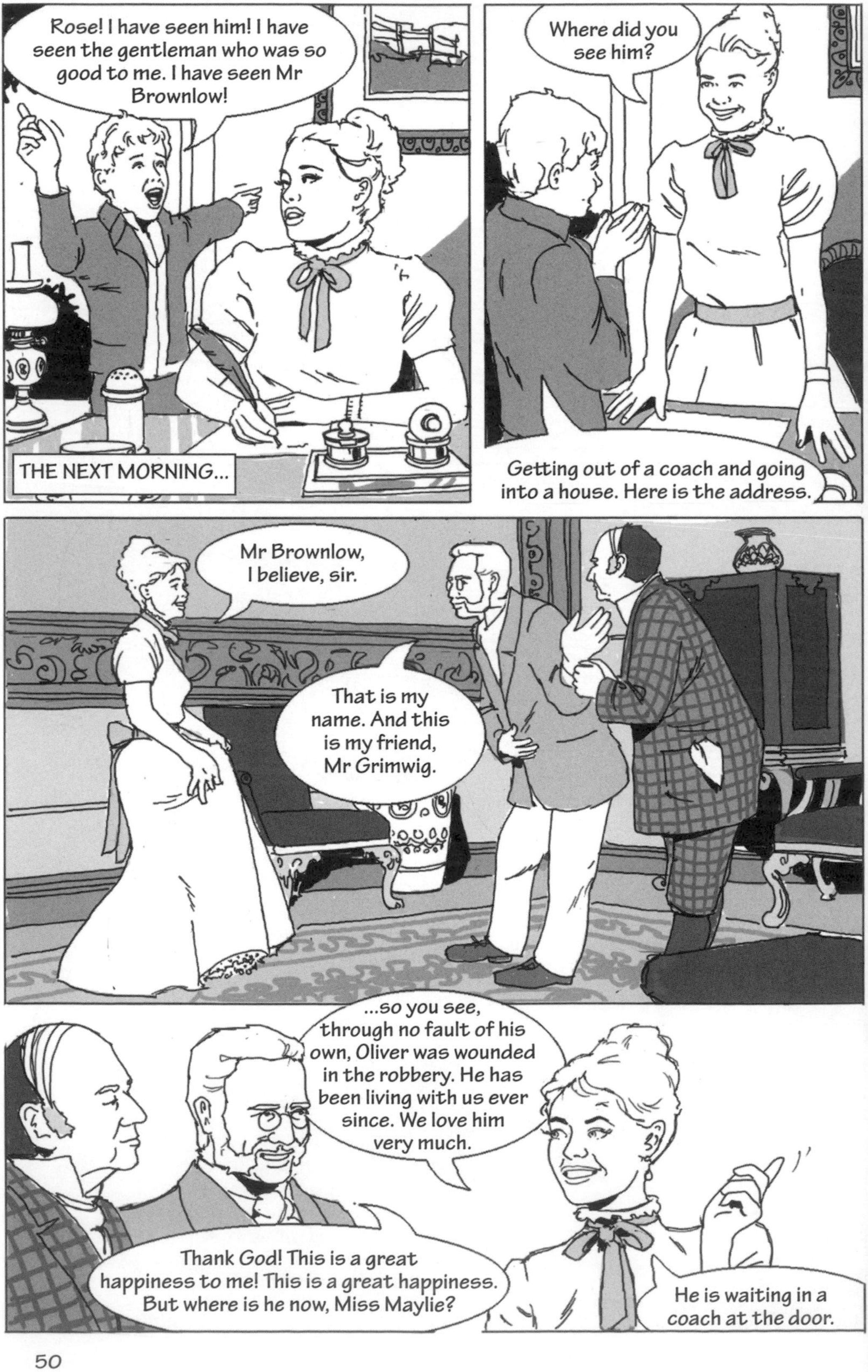
Rose! I have seen him! I have seen the gentleman who was so good to me. I have seen Mr Brownlow!
THE NEXT MORNING...
Where did you see him?
Getting out of a coach and going into a house. Here is the address.
Mr Brownlow, I believe, sir.
That is my name. And this is my friend, Mr Grimwig.
...so you see, through no fault of his own, Oliver was wounded in the robbery. He has been living with us ever since. We love him very much.
Thank God! This is a great happiness to me! This is a great happiness. But where is he now, Miss Maylie?
He is waiting in a coach at the door.

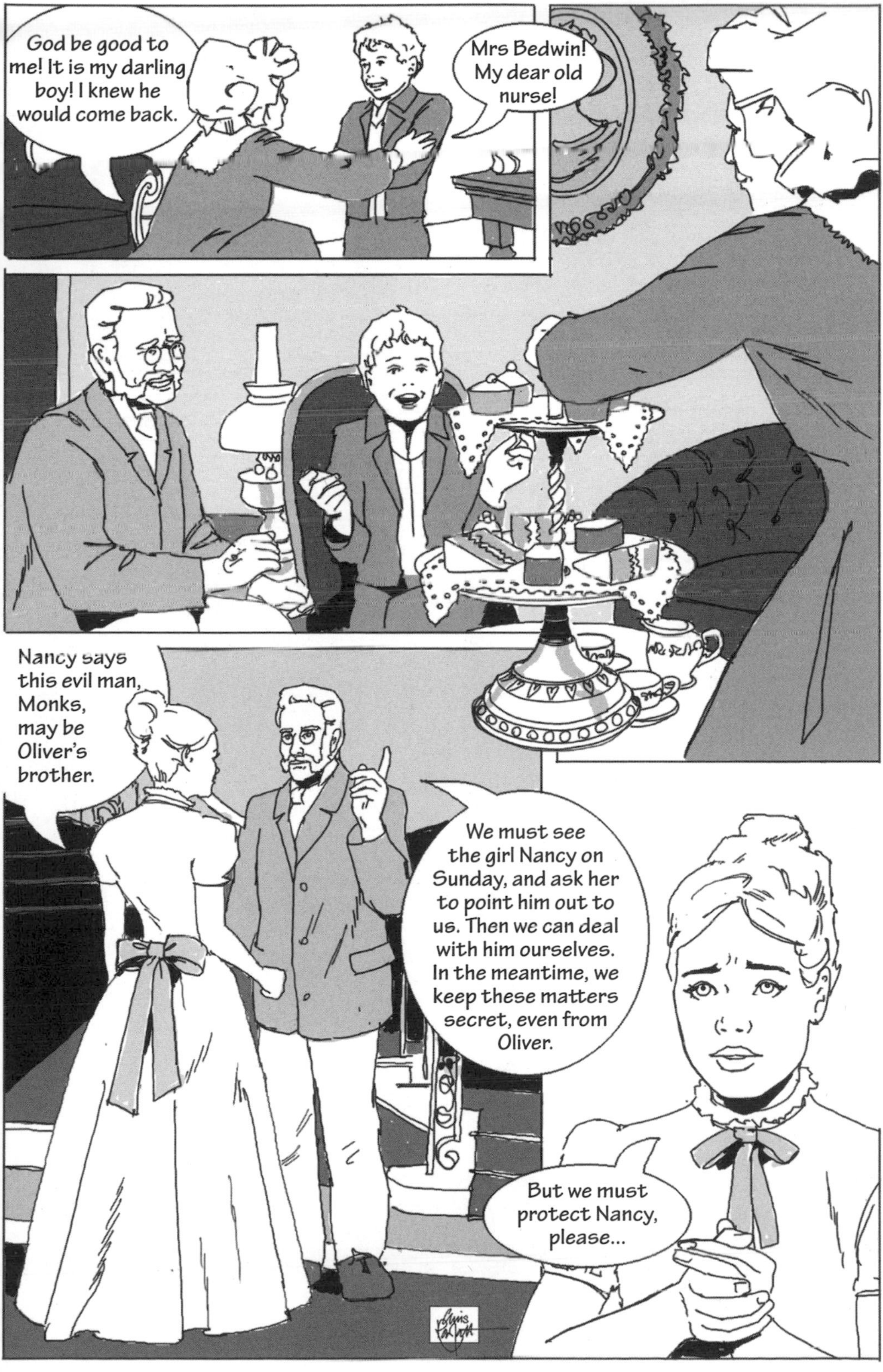
God be good to me! It is my darling boy! I knew he would come back.
Mrs Bedwin! My dear old nurse!
Nancy says this evil man, Monks, may be Oliver's brother.
We must see the girl Nancy on Sunday, and ask her to point him out to us. Then we can deal with him ourselves. In the meantime, we keep these matters secret, even from Oliver.
But we must protect Nancy, please...

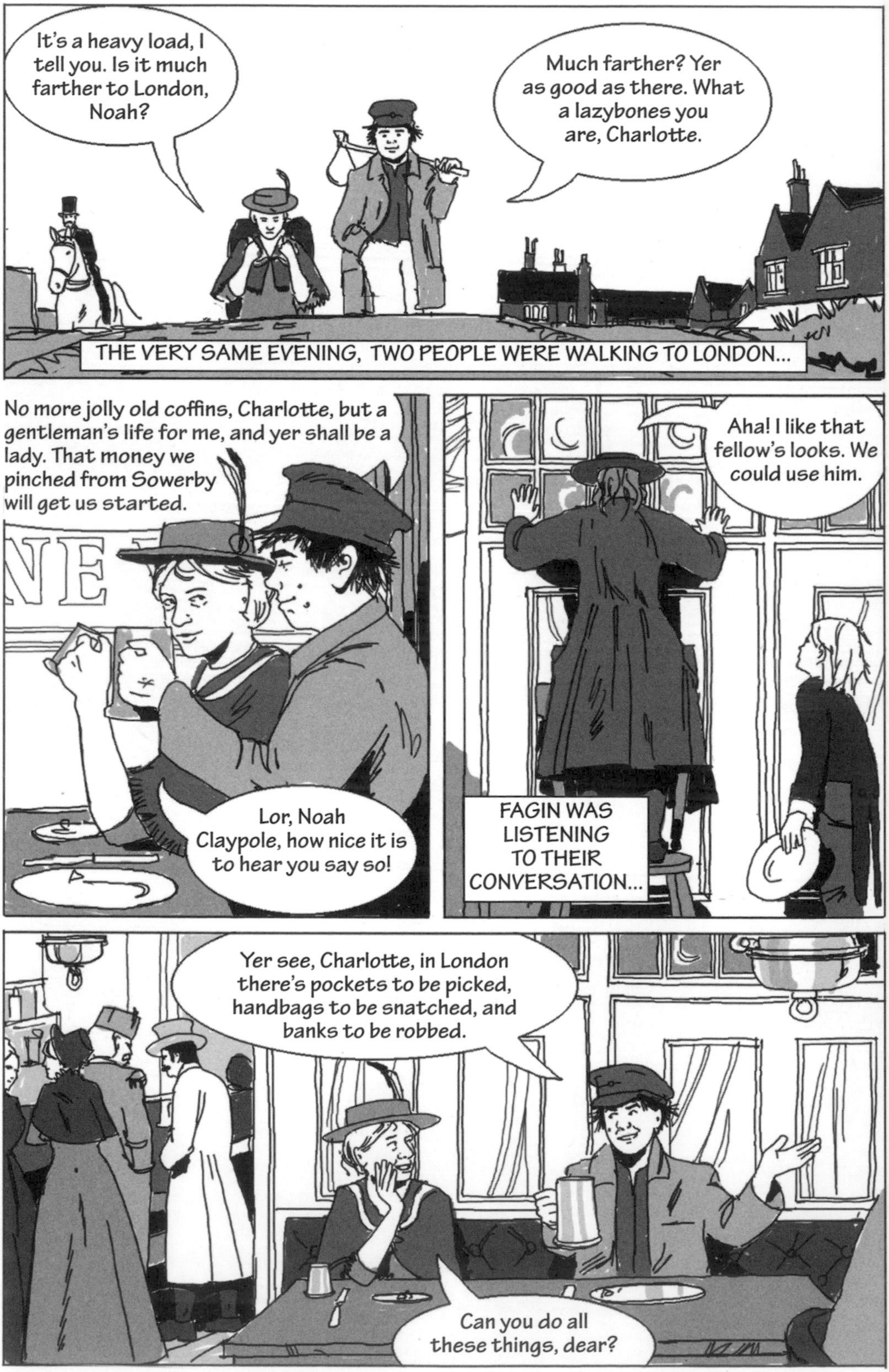

It's a heavy load, I tell you. Is it much farther to London, Noah?
Much farther? Yer as good as there. What a lazybones you are, Charlotte.
THE VERY SAME EVENING, TWO PEOPLE WERE WALKING TO LONDON...
No more jolly old coffins, Charlotte, but a gentleman's life for me, and yer shall be a lady. That money we pinched from Sowerby will get us started.
Lor, Noah Claypole, how nice it is to hear you say so!
Aha! I like that fellow's looks. We could use him.
FAGIN WAS LISTENING TO THEIR CONVERSATION...
Yer see, Charlotte, in London there's pockets to be picked, handbags to be snatched, and banks to be robbed.
Can you do all these things, dear?

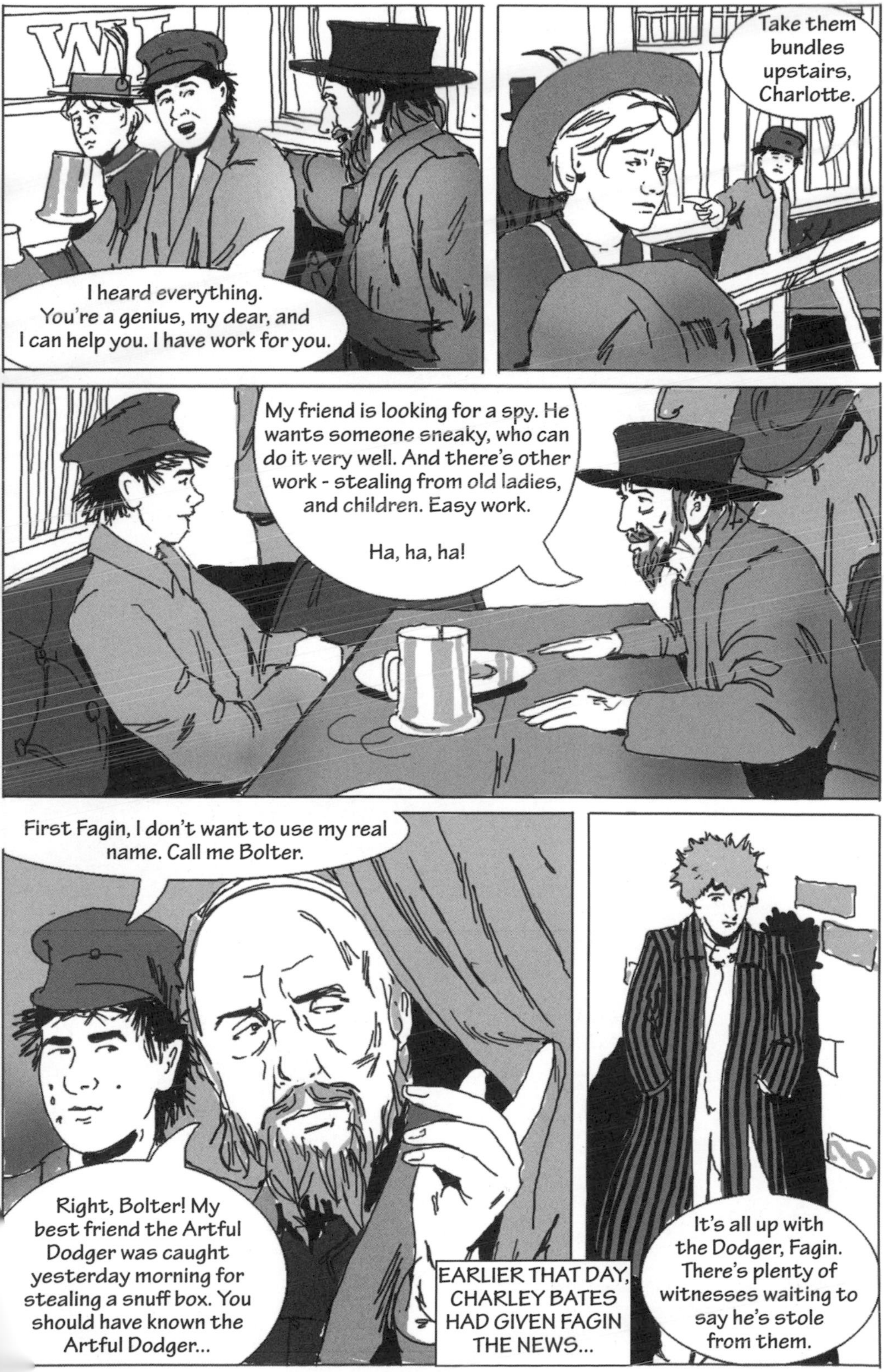
I heard everything. You're a genius, my dear, and I can help you. I have work for you.
Take them bundles upstairs, Charlotte.
My friend is looking for a spy. He wants someone sneaky, who can do it very well. And there's other work - stealing from old ladies, and children. Easy work.
Ha, ha, ha!
First Fagin, I don't want to use my real name. Call me Bolter.
Right, Bolter! My best friend the Artful Dodger was caught yesterday morning for stealing a snuff box. You should have known the Artful Dodger...
EARLIER THAT DAY, CHARLEY BATES HAD GIVEN FAGIN THE NEWS...
It's all up with the Dodger, Fagin. There's plenty of witnesses waiting to say he's stole from them.

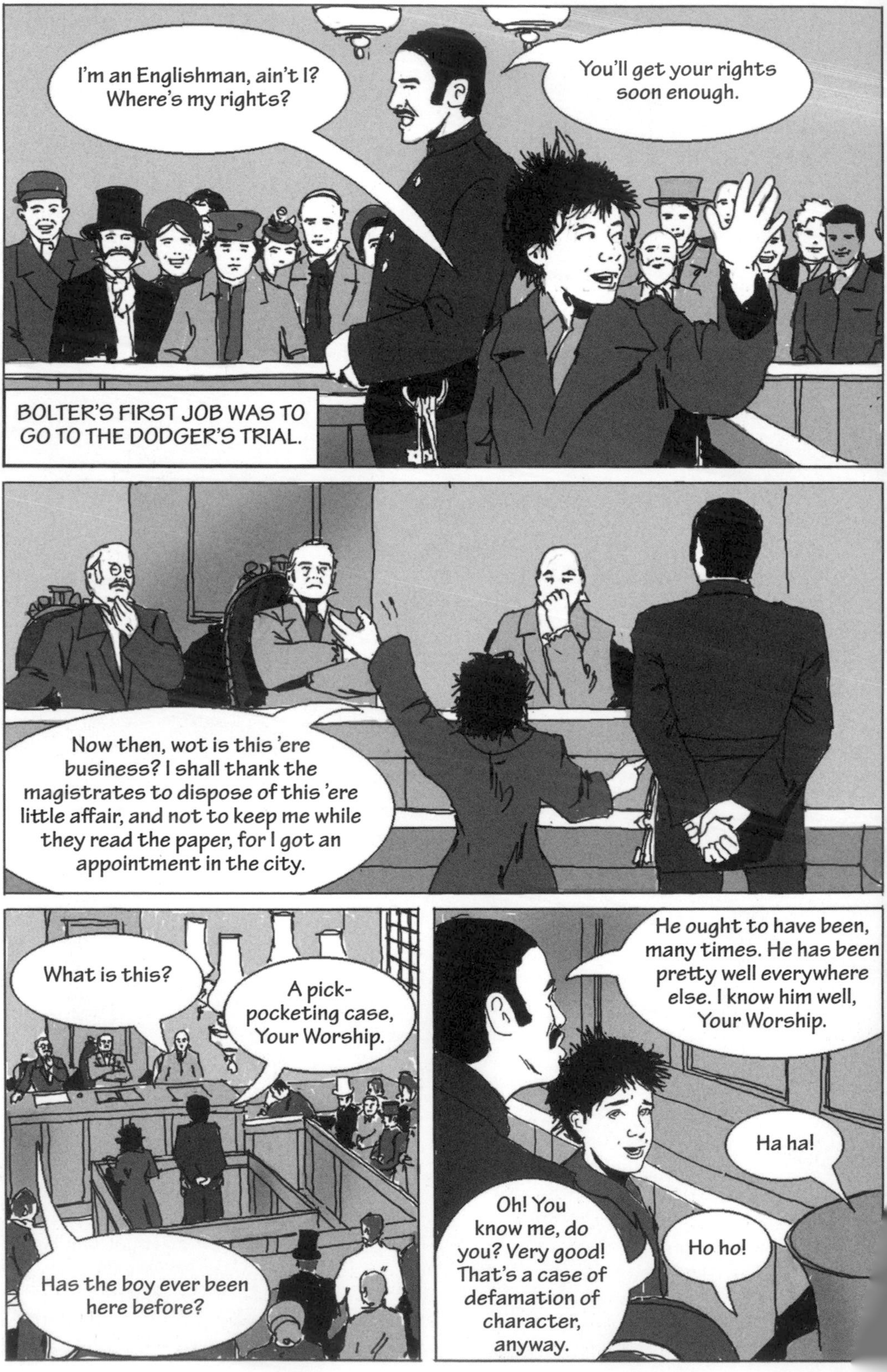
I'm an Englishman, ain't I? Where's my rights?
You'll get your rights soon enough.
BOLTER'S FIRST JOB WAS TO GO TO THE DODGER'S TRIAL.
Now then, wot is this 'ere business? I shall thank the magistrates to dispose of this 'ere little affair, and not to keep me while they read the paper, for I got an appointment in the city.
What is this?
A pick-pocketing case, Your Worship.
Has the boy ever been here before?
He ought to have been, many times. He has been pretty well everywhere else. I know him well, Your Worship.
Oh! You know me, do you? Very good! That's a case of defamation of character, anyway.
Ha ha!
Ho ho!

I saw him stealing from a market stall, but he's fast. He got away.

He stole my best lace handkerchief.

He grabbed my handbag and ran away. No one could catch him.

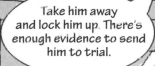

Take him away and lock him up. There's enough evidence to send him to trial.

You'll pay for this, my fine fellers. I wouldn't go free now, if you was to fall down on your knees and ask me. Here, carry me off to prison! Take me away!

COURT

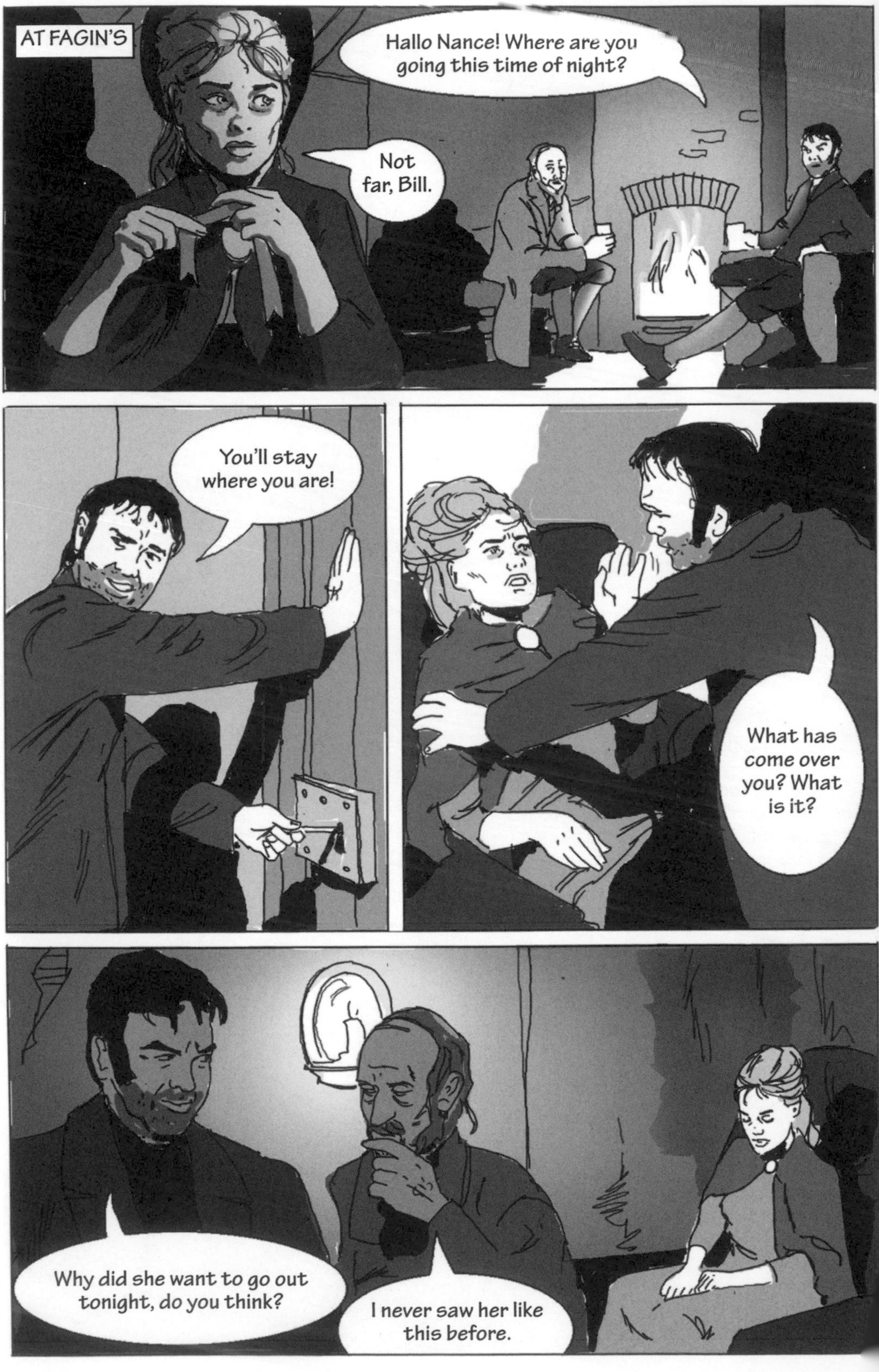
AT FAGIN'S
Hallo Nance! Where are you going this time of night?
Not far, Bill.
You'll stay where you are!
What has come over you? What is it?
Why did she want to go out tonight, do you think?
I never saw her like this before.

Bolter, I want you to follow that woman. Be very careful. She's one of us. I want to know where she goes, who she sees, even what she says. I'll pay you well.
A WEEK LATER, NANCY FINALLY MANAGED TO SLIP OUT...
Quick - after her!
Not here, I'm afraid to speak to you here. Come down these steps.
You must tell me where to find this man Monks. We must get the truth from him.
If I help you, you must keep me out of it. Never tell anyone - or they'll kill me, Miss Maylie!
We promise. We'll tell no one.
From your description, I think I know the man. We shall see. We shall see...

But what can we do to help you, young woman? You have helped us. We must help you.
I just want to help the boy, Oliver. You can do nothing to help me. I am past all help. Bless you! God bless you! Good night, good night.
Tell Bill what you just told me - about Nancy. How you followed her to London Bridge where she met two people - a gentleman and a lady. Right?
So she did.
And she told them about Monks, what he looked like and where to find him, and us too, right?
That's just what it was!
Hell's fire! Let me get at Nancy!
You won't be too violent, Bill?

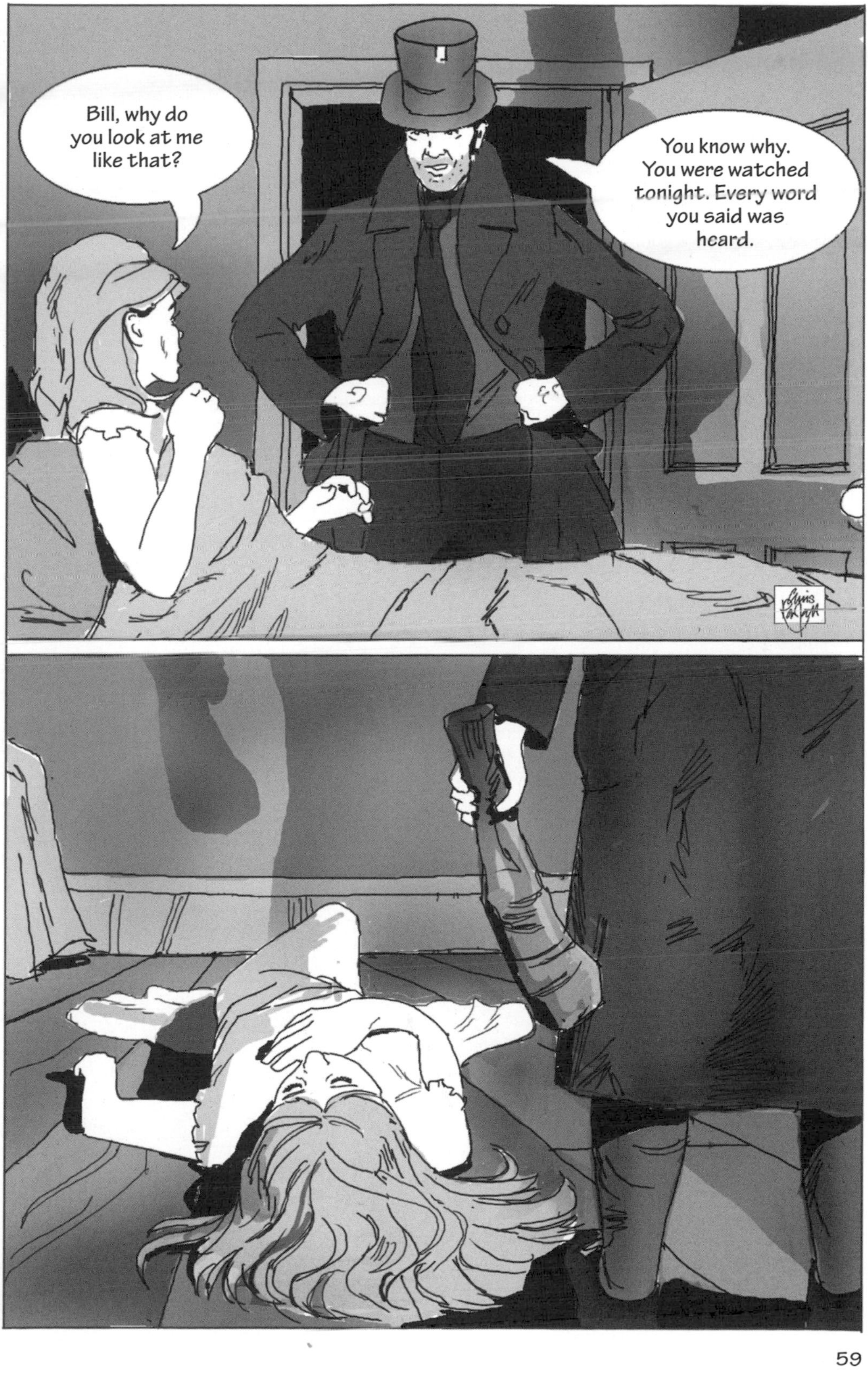
Bill, why do you look at me like that?
You know why. You were watched tonight. Every word you said was heard.

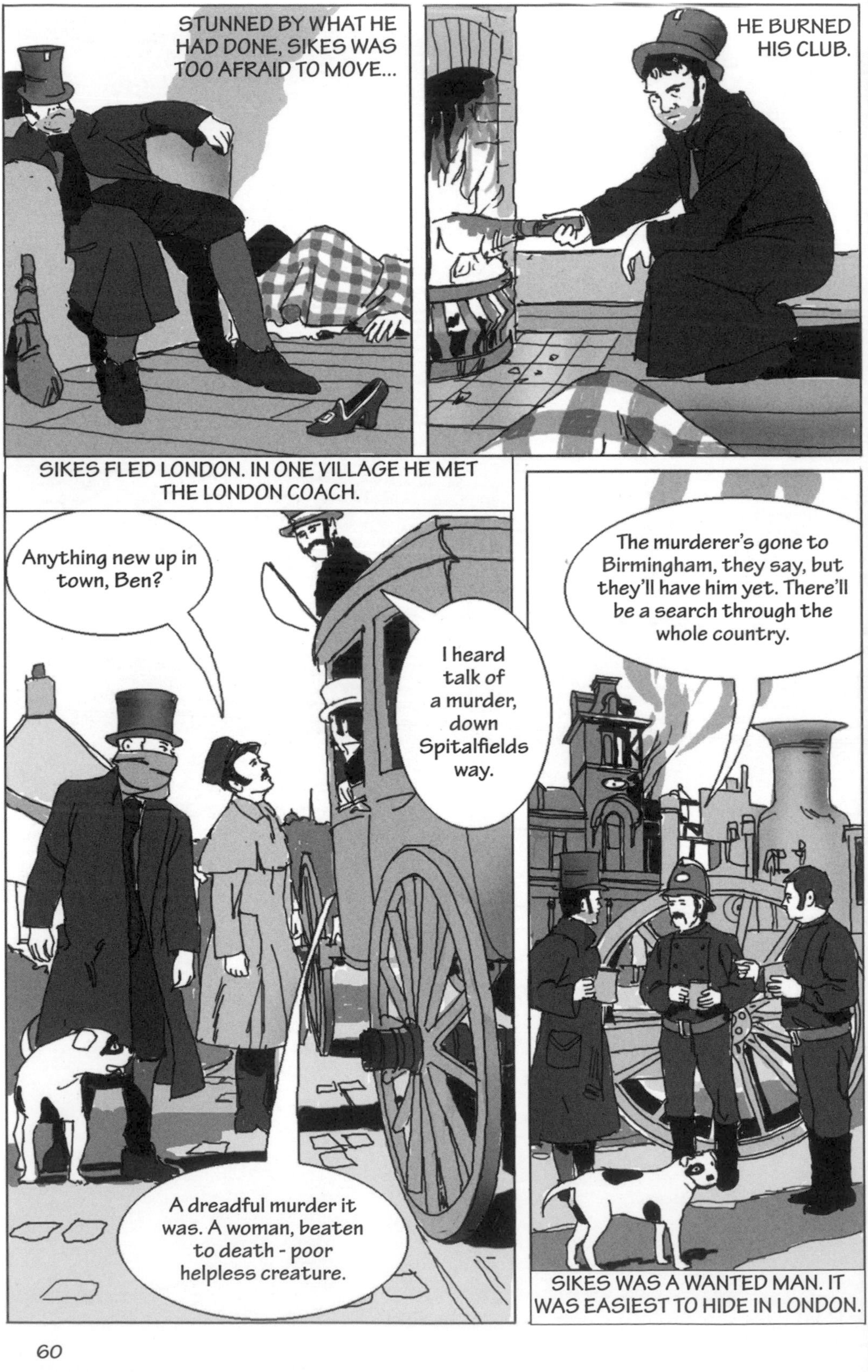
STUNNED BY WHAT HE HAD DONE, SIKES WAS TOO AFRAID TO MOVE...
HE BURNED HIS CLUB.
SIKES FLED LONDON. IN ONE VILLAGE HE MET THE LONDON COACH.
Anything new up in town, Ben?
I heard talk of a murder, down Spitalfields way.
A dreadful murder it was. A woman, beaten to death - poor helpless creature.
The murderer's gone to Birmingham, they say, but they'll have him yet. There'll be a search through the whole country.
SIKES WAS A WANTED MAN. IT WAS EASIEST TO HIDE IN LONDON.

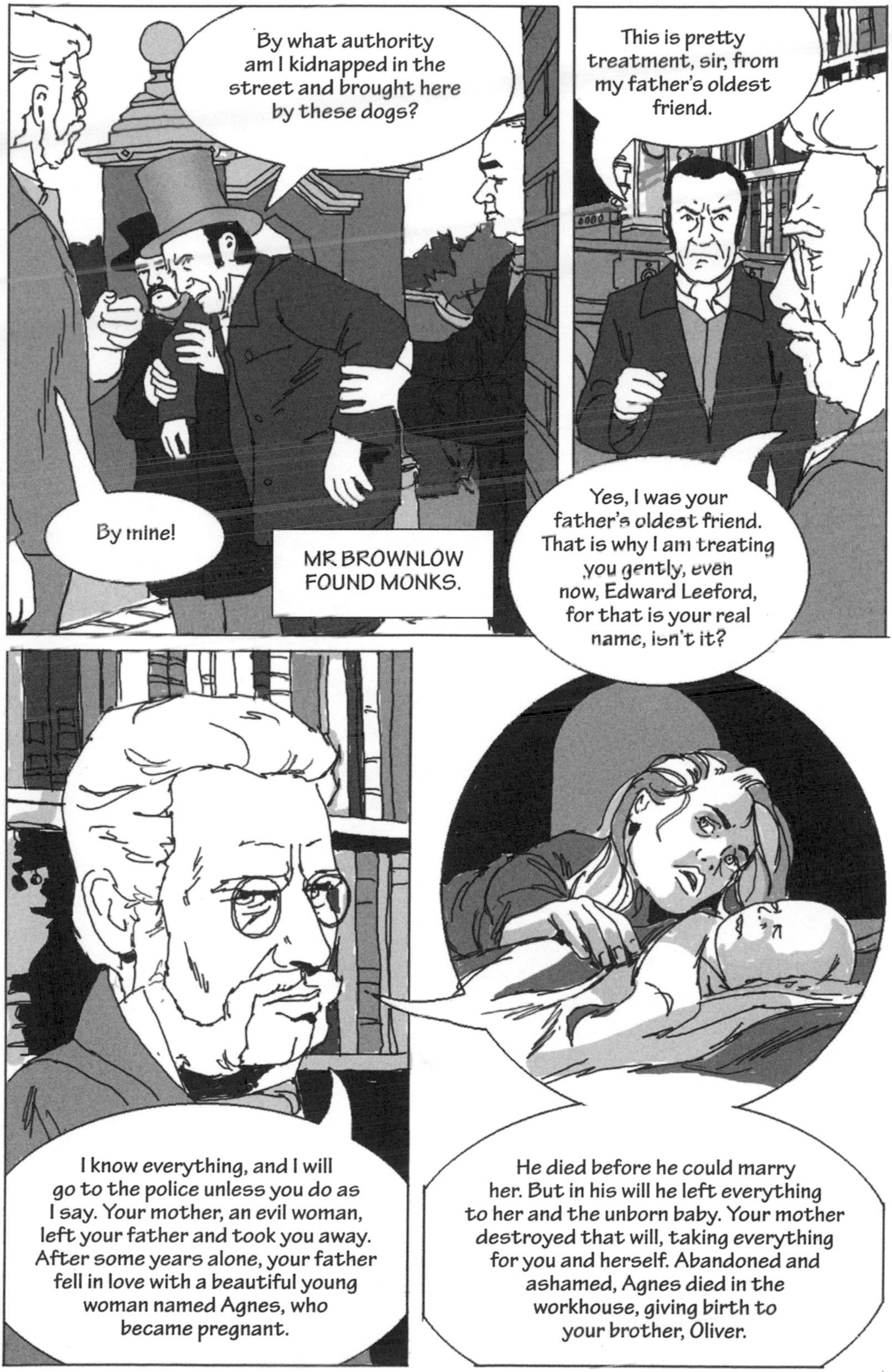
By what authority am I kidnapped in the street and brought here by these dogs?
By mine!
MR BROWNLOW FOUND MONKS.
This is pretty treatment, sir, from my father's oldest friend.
Yes, I was your father's oldest friend. That is why I am treating you gently, even now, Edward Leeford, for that is your real name, isn't it?
I know everything, and I will go to the police unless you do as I say. Your mother, an evil woman, left your father and took you away. After some years alone, your father fell in love with a beautiful young woman named Agnes, who became pregnant.
He died before he could marry her. But in his will he left everything to her and the unborn baby. Your mother destroyed that will, taking everything for you and herself. Abandoned and ashamed, Agnes died in the workhouse, giving birth to your brother, Oliver.

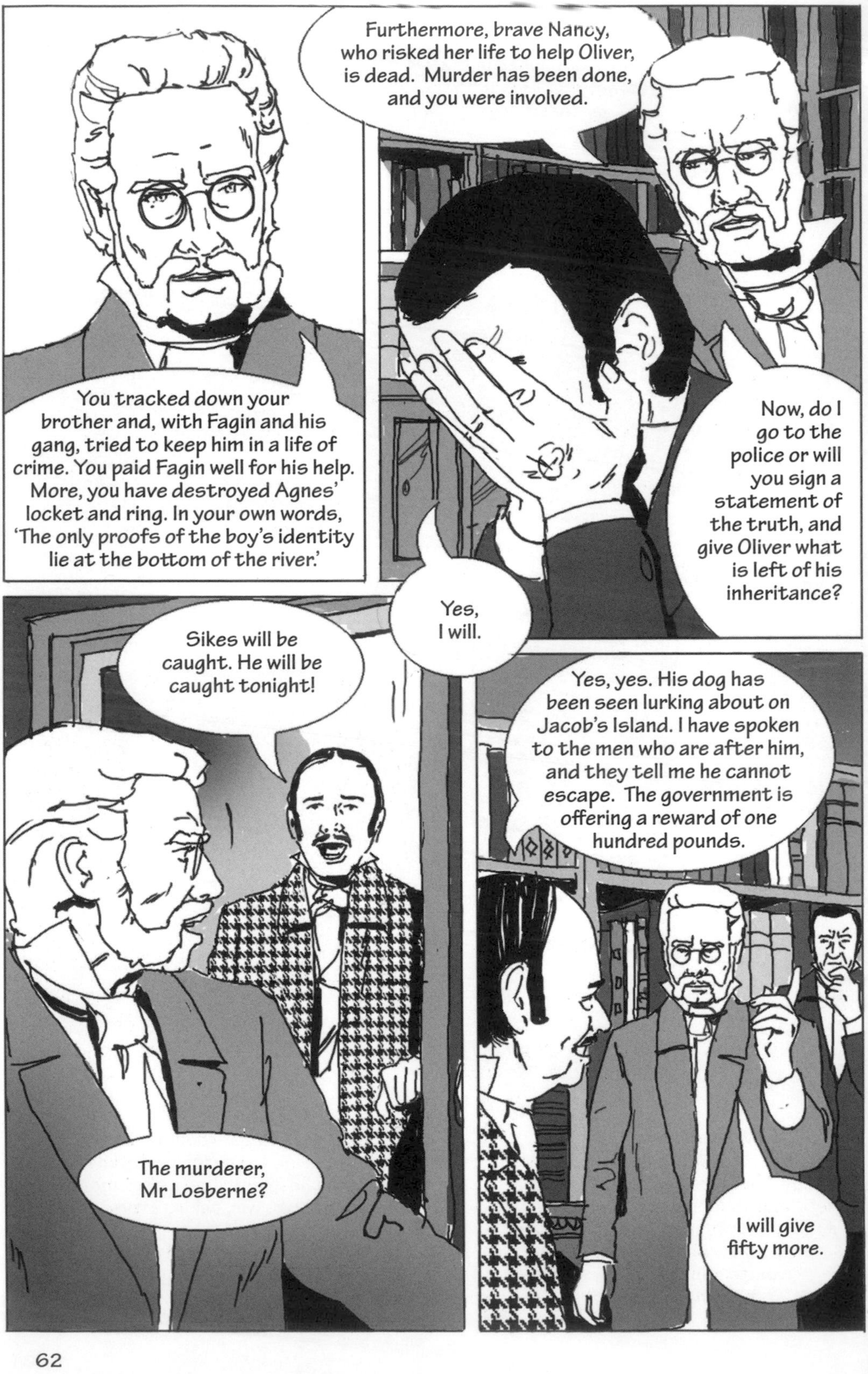
You tracked down your brother and, with Fagin and his gang, tried to keep him in a life of crime. You paid Fagin well for his help. More, you have destroyed Agnes' locket and ring. In your own words, 'The only proofs of the boy's identity lie at the bottom of the river.'
Furthermore, brave Nancy, who risked her life to help Oliver, is dead. Murder has been done, and you were involved.
Now, do I go to the police or will you sign a statement of the truth, and give Oliver what is left of his inheritance?
Yes, I will.
Sikes will be caught. He will be caught tonight!
The murderer, Mr Losberne?
Yes, yes. His dog has been seen lurking about on Jacob's Island. I have spoken to the men who are after him, and they tell me he cannot escape. The government is offering a reward of one hundred pounds.
I will give fifty more.

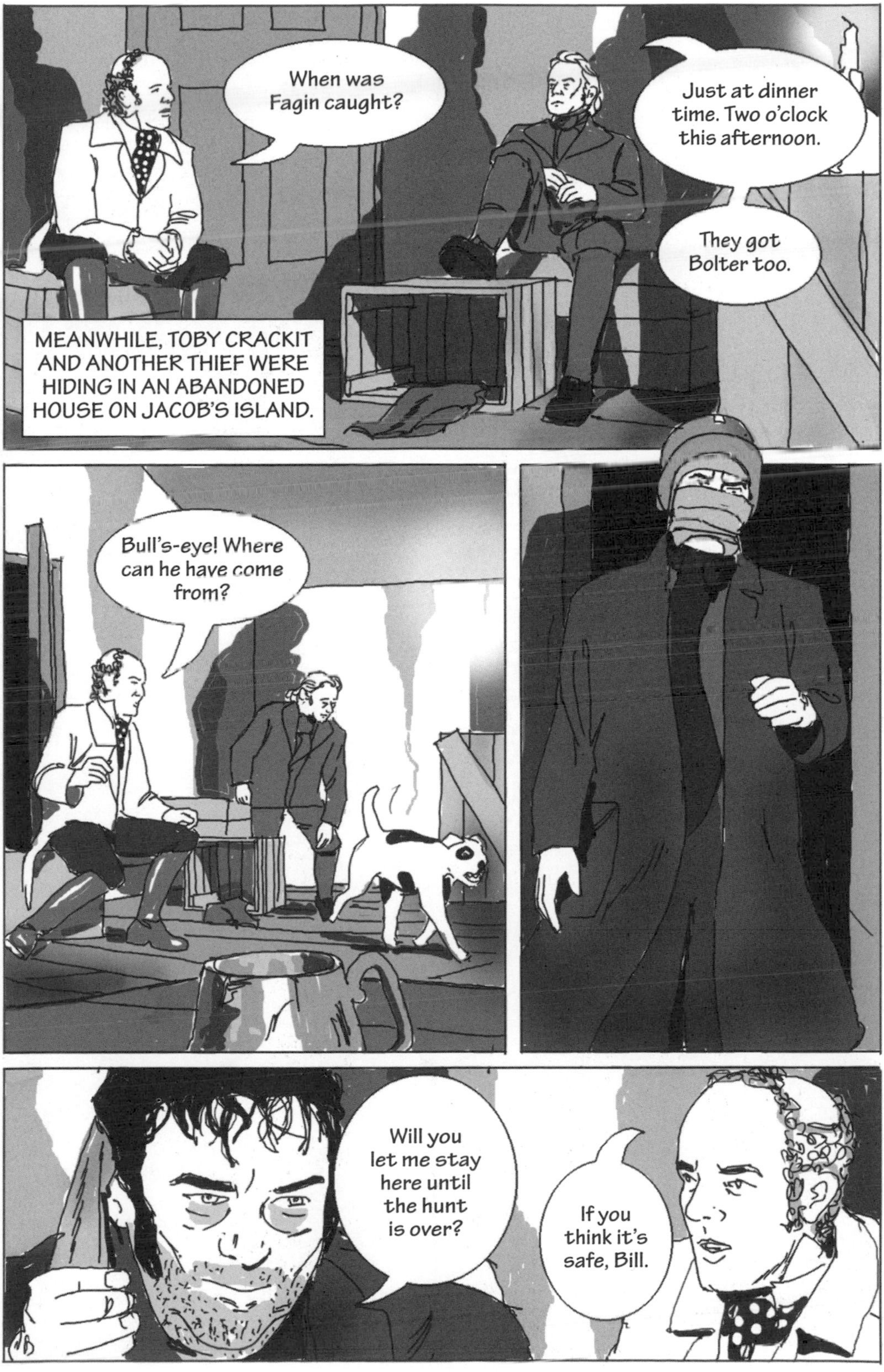
MEANWHILE, TOBY CRACKIT AND ANOTHER THIEF WERE HIDING IN AN ABANDONED HOUSE ON JACOB'S ISLAND.
When was Fagin caught?
Just at dinner time. Two o'clock this afternoon.
They got Bolter too.
Bull's-eye! Where can he have come from?
Will you let me stay here until the hunt is over?
If you think it's safe, Bill.

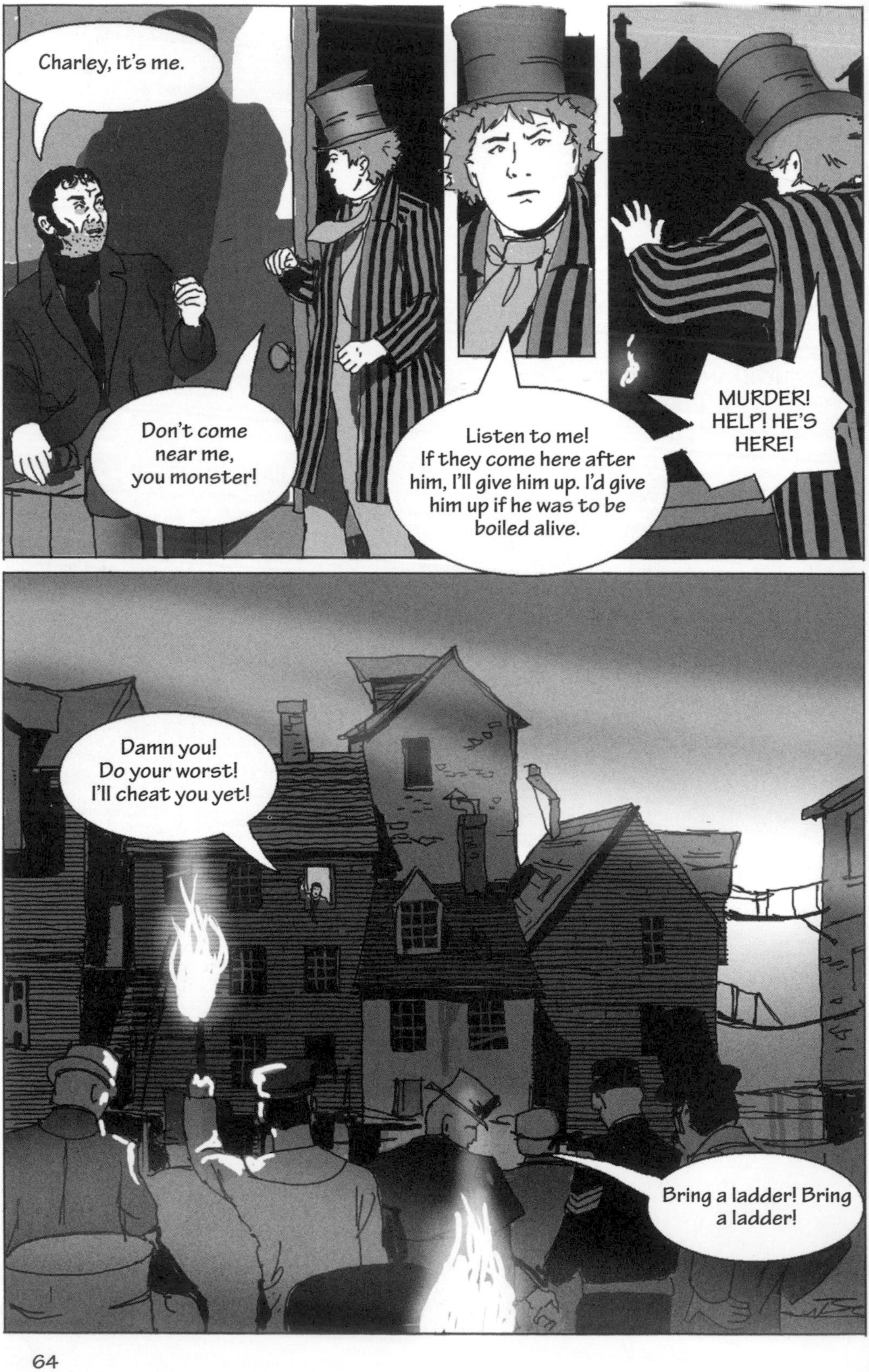
Charley, it's me.
Don't come near me, you monster!
Listen to me! If they come here after him, I'll give him up. I'd give him up if he was to be boiled alive.
MURDER! HELP! HE'S HERE!
Damn you! Do your worst! I'll cheat you yet!
Bring a ladder! Bring a ladder!

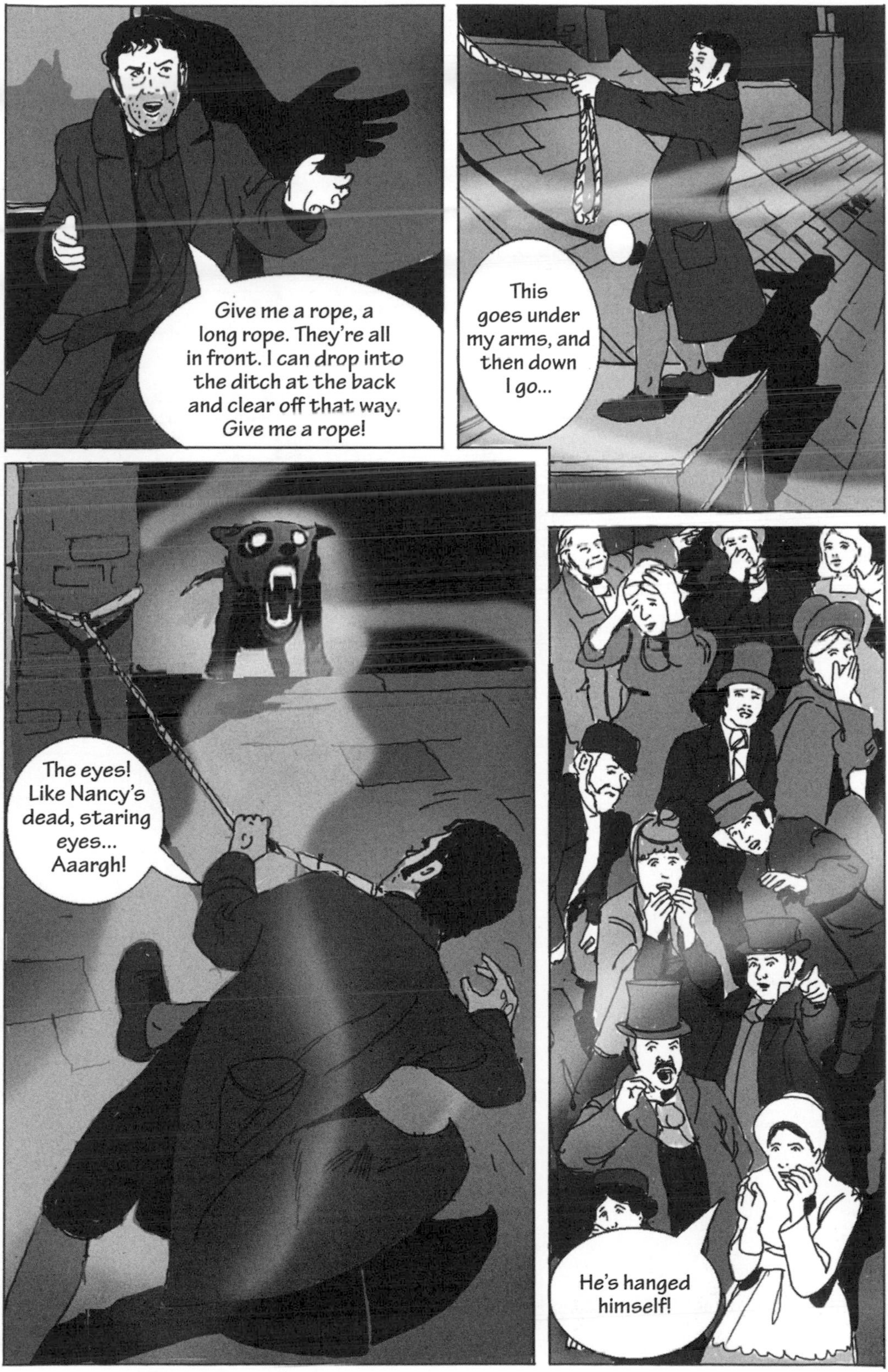
Give me a rope, a long rope. They're all in front. I can drop into the ditch at the back and clear off that way. Give me a rope!
This goes under my arms, and then down I go...
The eyes! Like Nancy's dead, staring eyes... Aaargh!
He's hanged himself!

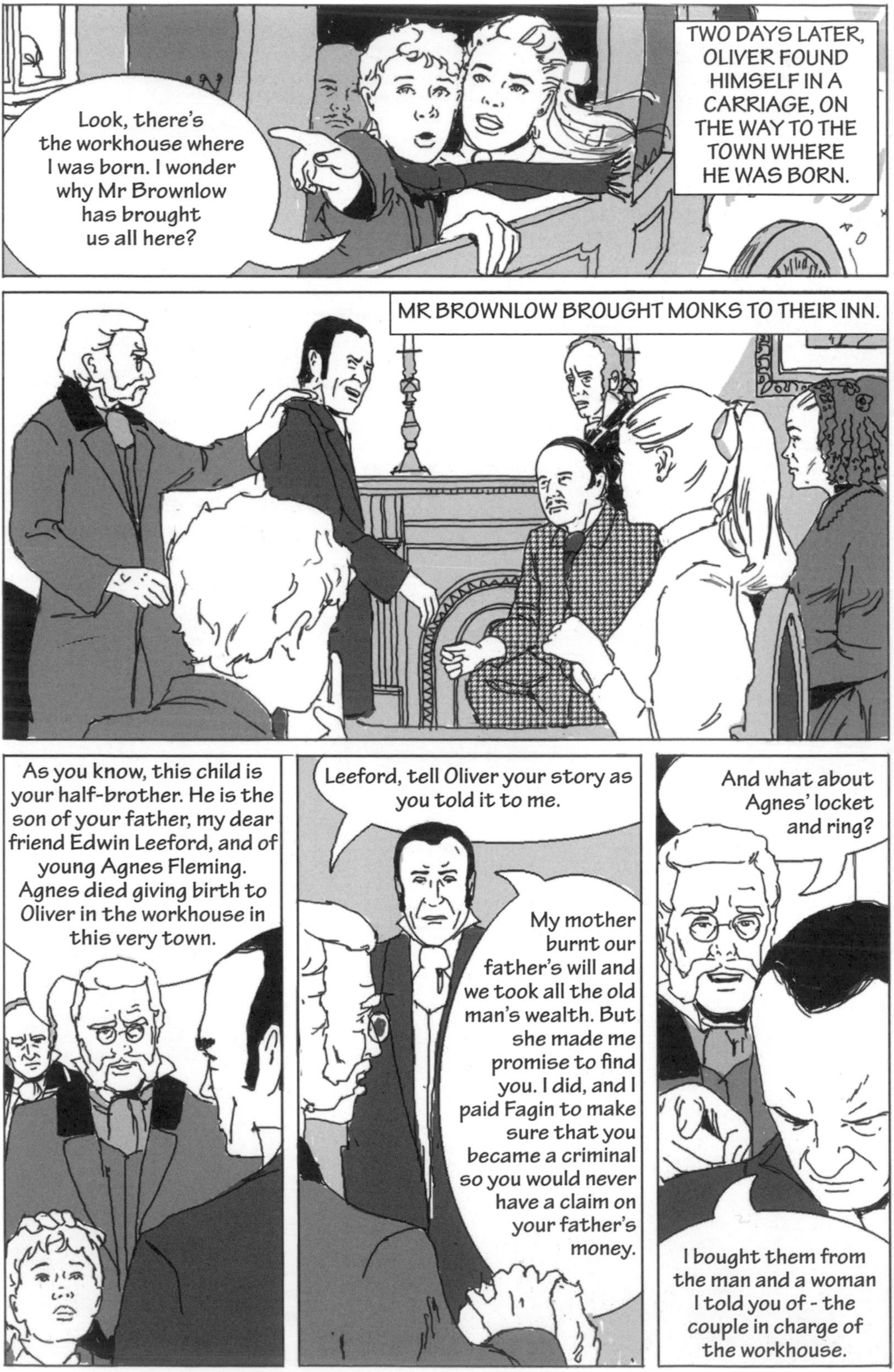
TWO DAYS LATER, OLIVER FOUND HIMSELF IN A CARRIAGE, ON THE WAY TO THE TOWN WHERE HE WAS BORN.
Look, there's the workhouse where I was born. I wonder why Mr Brownlow has brought us all here?
MR BROWNLOW BROUGHT MONKS TO THEIR INN.
As you know, this child is your half-brother. He is the son of your father, my dear friend Edwin Leeford, and of young Agnes Fleming. Agnes died giving birth to Oliver in the workhouse in this very town.
Leeford, tell Oliver your story as you told it to me.
My mother burnt our father's will and we took all the old man's wealth. But she made me promise to find you. I did, and I paid Fagin to make sure that you became a criminal so you would never have a claim on your father's money.
And what about Agnes' locket and ring?
I bought them from the man and a woman I told you of - the couple in charge of the workhouse.

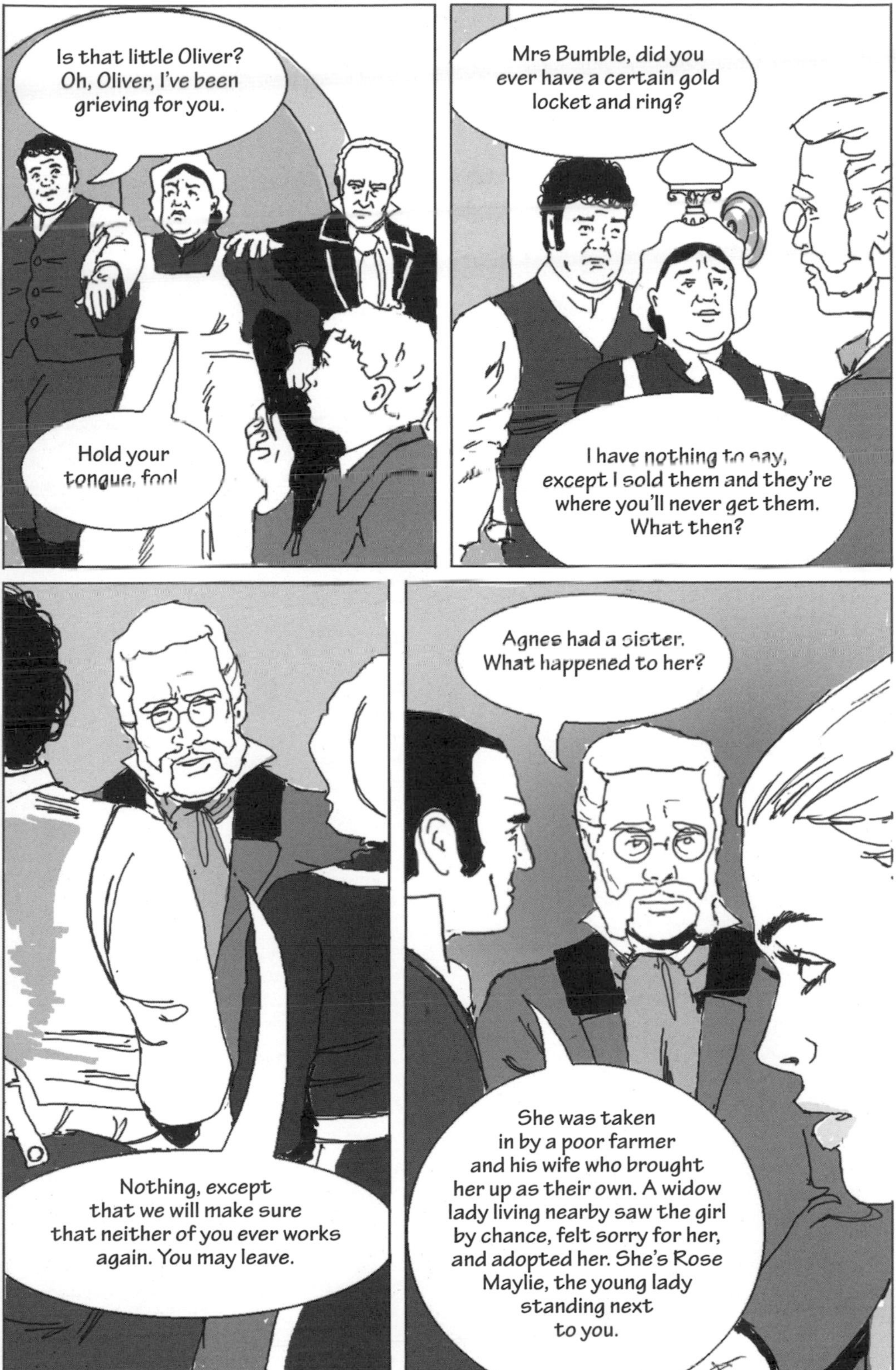
Is that little Oliver? Oh, Oliver, I've been grieving for you.
Hold your tongue, fool
Mrs Bumble, did you ever have a certain gold locket and ring?
I have nothing to say, except I sold them and they're where you'll never get them. What then?
Nothing, except that we will make sure that neither of you ever works again. You may leave.
Agnes had a sister. What happened to her?
She was taken in by a poor farmer and his wife who brought her up as their own. A widow lady living nearby saw the girl by chance, felt sorry for her, and adopted her. She's Rose Maylie, the young lady standing next to you.

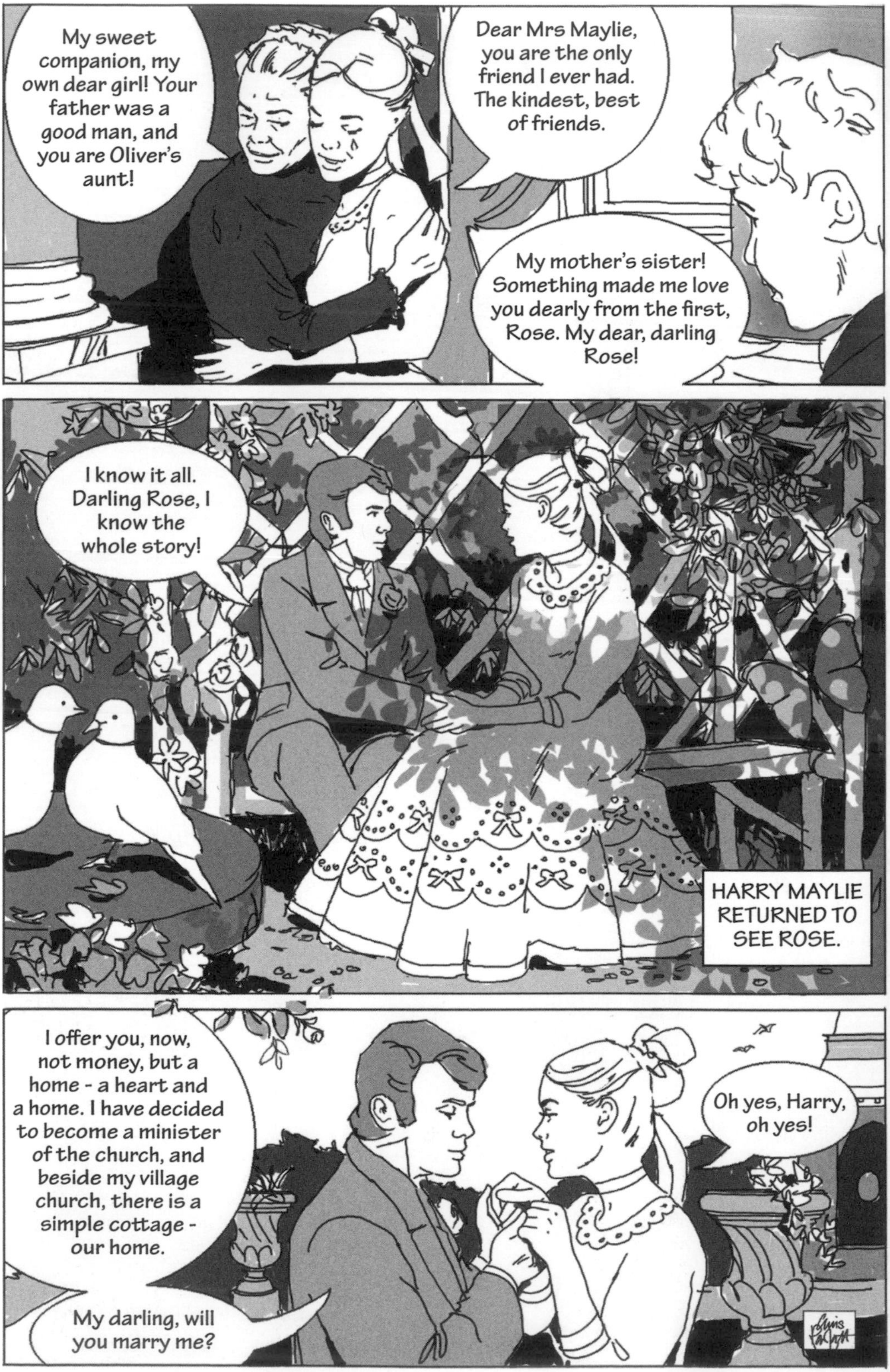
My sweet companion, my own dear girl! Your father was a good man, and you are Oliver's aunt!
Dear Mrs Maylie, you are the only friend I ever had. The kindest, best of friends.
My mother's sister! Something made me love you dearly from the first, Rose. My dear, darling Rose!
HARRY MAYLIE RETURNED TO SEE ROSE.
I know it all. Darling Rose, I know the whole story!
I offer you, now, not money, but a home - a heart and a home. I have decided to become a minister of the church, and beside my village church, there is a simple cottage - our home.
My darling, will you marry me?
Oh yes, Harry, oh yes!

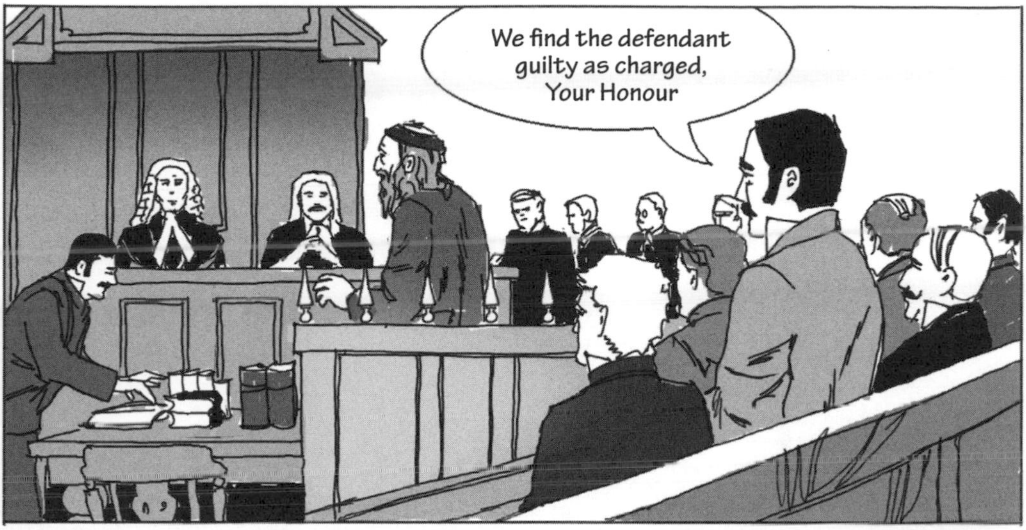
We find the defendant guilty as charged, Your Honour

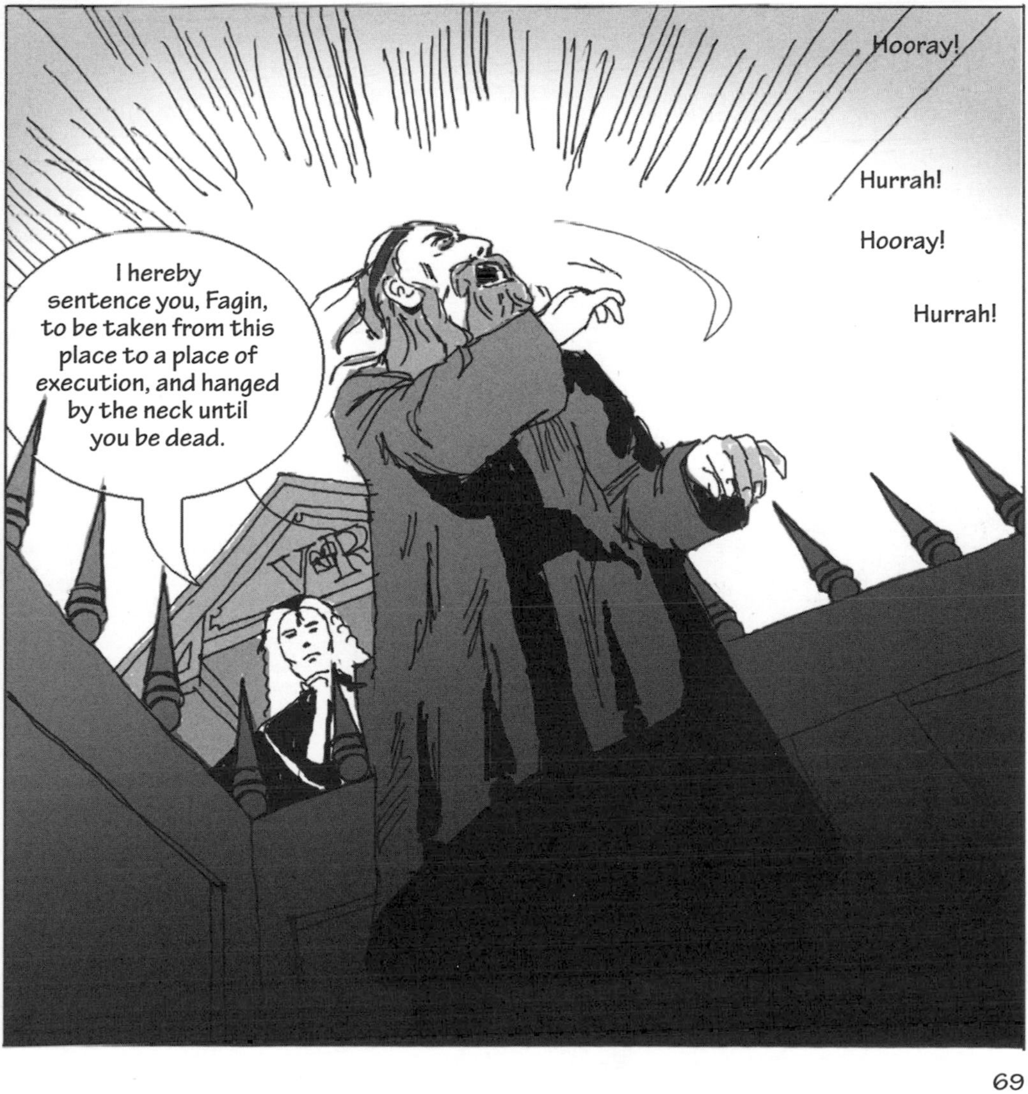
Hooray!
Hurrah!
Hooray!
Hurrah!
I hereby sentence you, Fagin, to be taken from this place to a place of execution, and hanged by the neck until you be dead.

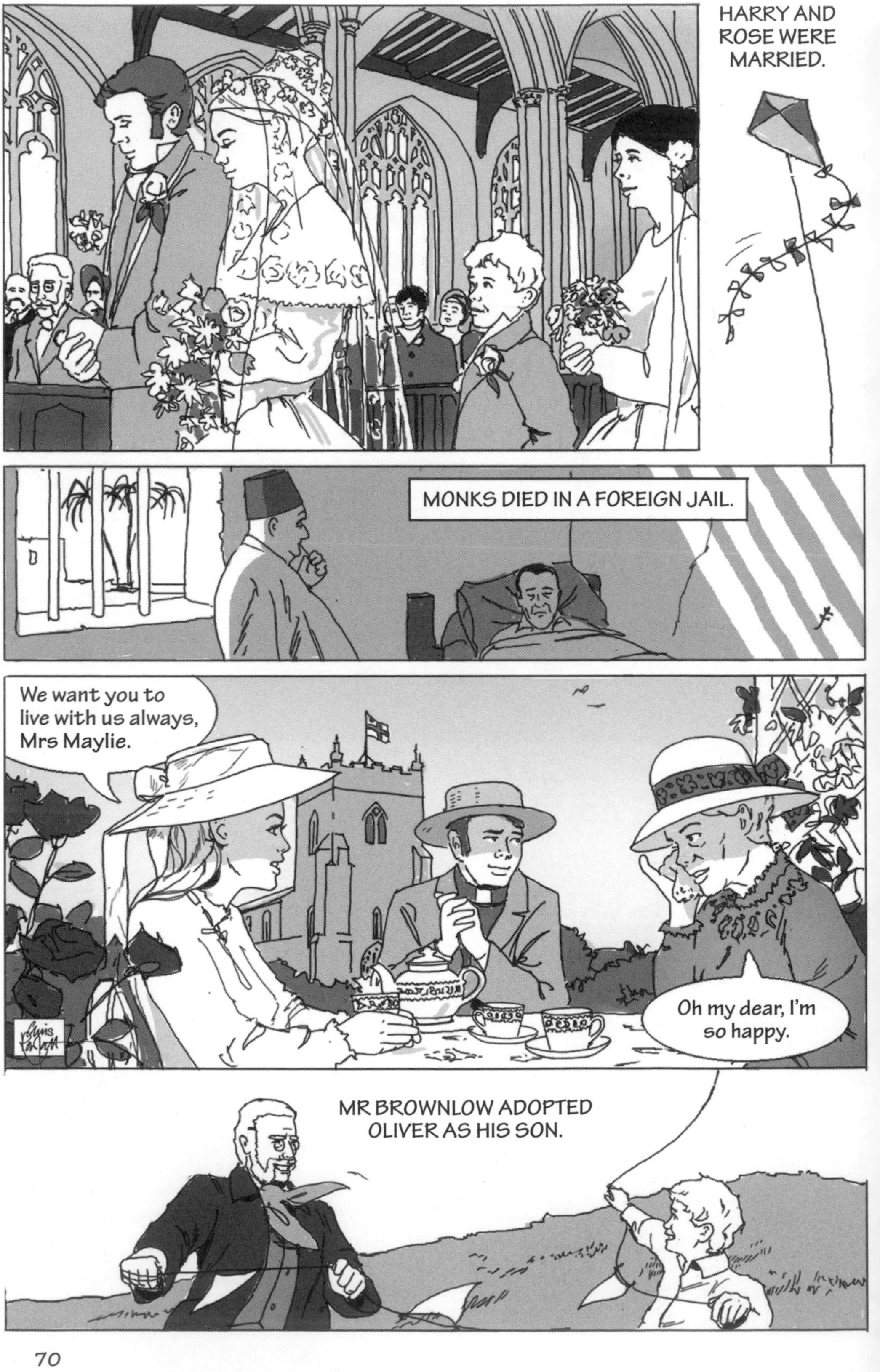
HARRY AND ROSE WERE MARRIED.
MONKS DIED IN A FOREIGN JAIL.
We want you to live with us always, Mrs Maylie.
Oh my dear, I'm so happy.
MR BROWNLOW ADOPTED OLIVER AS HIS SON.

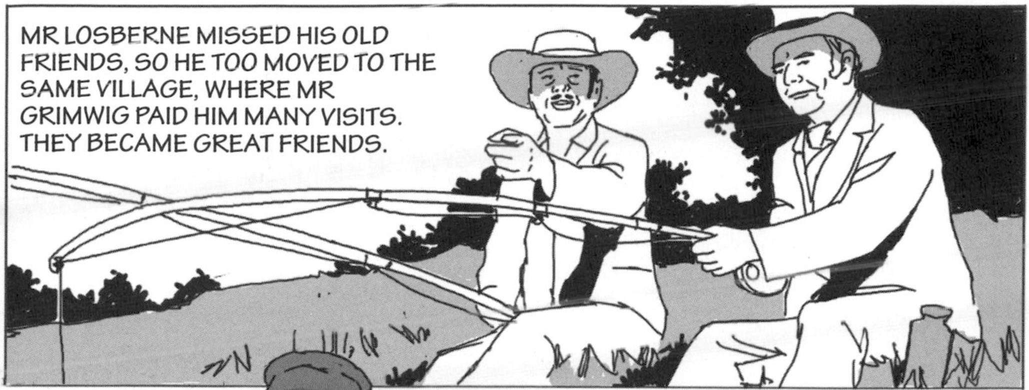
MR LOSBERNE MISSED HIS OLD FRIENDS, SO HE TOO MOVED TO THE SAME VILLAGE, WHERE MR GRIMWIG PAID HIM MANY VISITS. THEY BECAME GREAT FRIENDS.

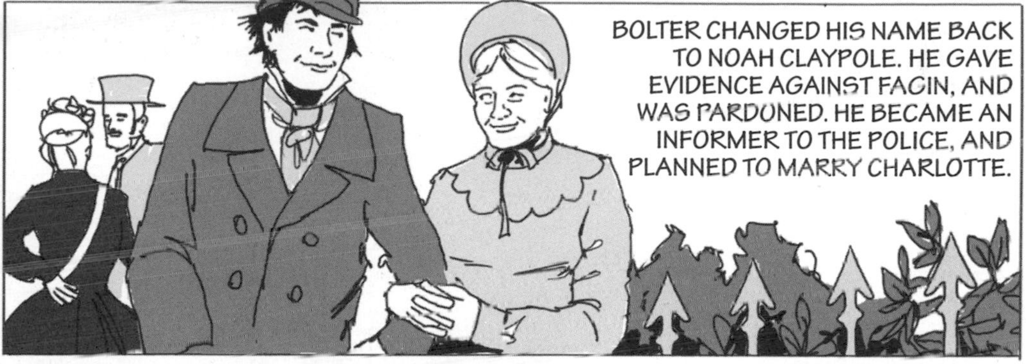
BOLTER CHANGED HIS NAME BACK TO NOAH CLAYPOLE. HE GAVE EVIDENCE AGAINST FAGIN, AND WAS PARDONED. HE BECAME AN INFORMER TO THE POLICE, AND PLANNED TO MARRY CHARLOTTE.

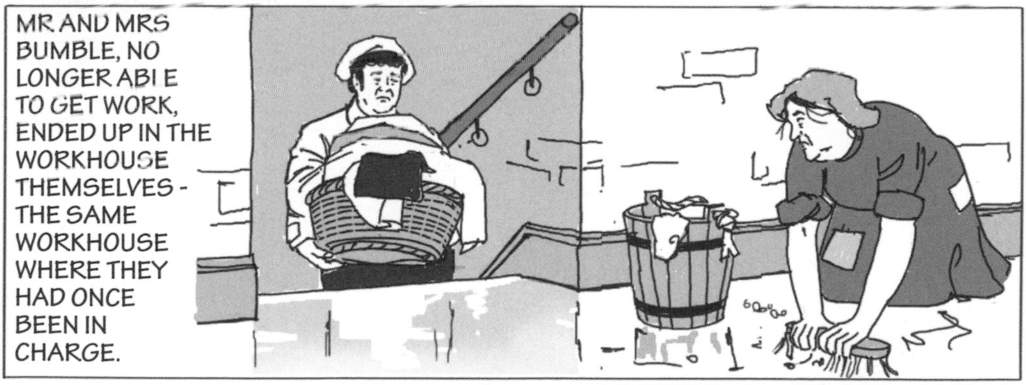
MR AND MRS BUMBLE, NO LONGER ABLE TO GET WORK, ENDED UP IN THE WORKHOUSE THEMSELVES - THE SAME WORKHOUSE WHERE THEY HAD ONCE BEEN IN CHARGE.

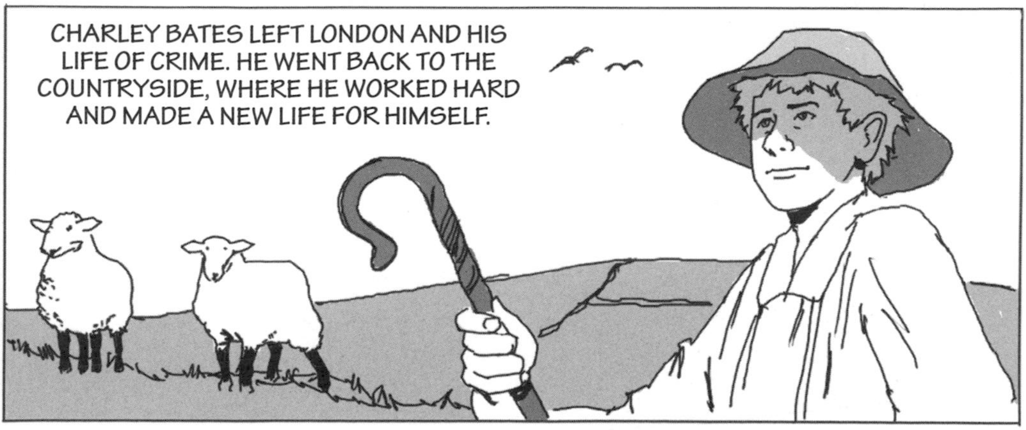
CHARLEY BATES LEFT LONDON AND HIS LIFE OF CRIME. HE WENT BACK TO THE COUNTRYSIDE, WHERE HE WORKED HARD AND MADE A NEW LIFE FOR HIMSELF.

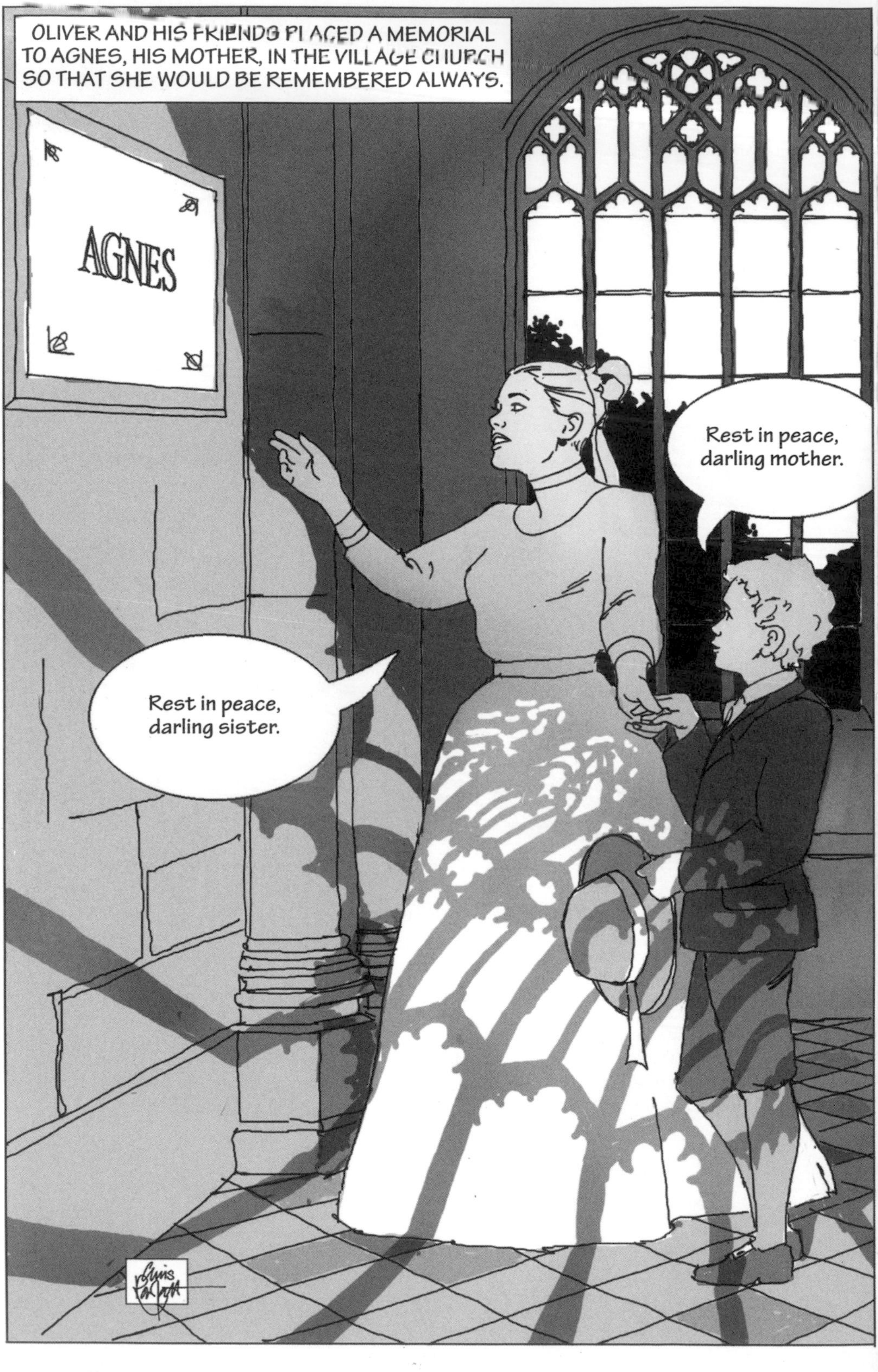
OLIVER AND HIS FRIENDS PLACED A MEMORIAL TO AGNES, HIS MOTHER, IN THE VILLAGE CHURCH SO THAT SHE WOULD BE REMEMBERED ALWAYS.
AGNES
Rest in peace, darling mother.
Rest in peace, darling sister.